Song for a Dark Queen

Chosen as a Children's Book of
the Year 1978

Listen now, for your sword is singing,
'I am the proud one, I that am sword to
a Queen . . .'

Since the day he had fashioned a sword out of a willow wand for the young Boudicca and, at her insistence, composed a victory song that was in part a lullaby for her, Cadwan the Harp had kept the record for his Queen. As Boudicca led the Iceni from victory to victory the first improvisation proved prophetic; then the light faded, leaving but one tragic course open to the dark queen . . .

Jacket illustration by Tudor Humphries

Some reviews of SONG FOR A DARK QUEEN

'. . . harsh and tender, strident and poetic, savage and gentle.'
Elaine Moss, *Children's Books of the Year 1978*

'All Rosemary Sutcliff's well-known skills are here . . . Masterly . . . skilful.'
Times Literary Supplement

'Exhilarating in colour and pace.'
The Sunday Times

'Rosemary Sutcliff tells her story with a poetic sense of time and place. It is not at all surprising that she won her Carnegie Medal.'
Books and Bookmen

SONG FOR A DARK QUEEN was joint winner of the Other Award in 1978.

Song for a Dark Queen

Rosemary Sutcliff

KNIGHT BOOKS
Hodder and Stoughton

First published 1978 by Pelham Books Ltd.

This edition first published by Knight Books 1980
Fourth impression 1984

British Library C.I.P.

Sutcliff, Rosemary
Song for a dark queen.
I. Title
823′.9′1J PZ7.S966

ISBN 0–340–24864–5

Printed and bound in Great Britain for
Hodder and Stoughton Paperbacks, a
division of Hodder and Stoughton Ltd.,
Mill Road, Dunton Green, Sevenoaks,
Kent (Editorial Office: 47 Bedford
Square, London, WC1 3DP) by
Cox & Wyman Ltd.,
Reading

Contents

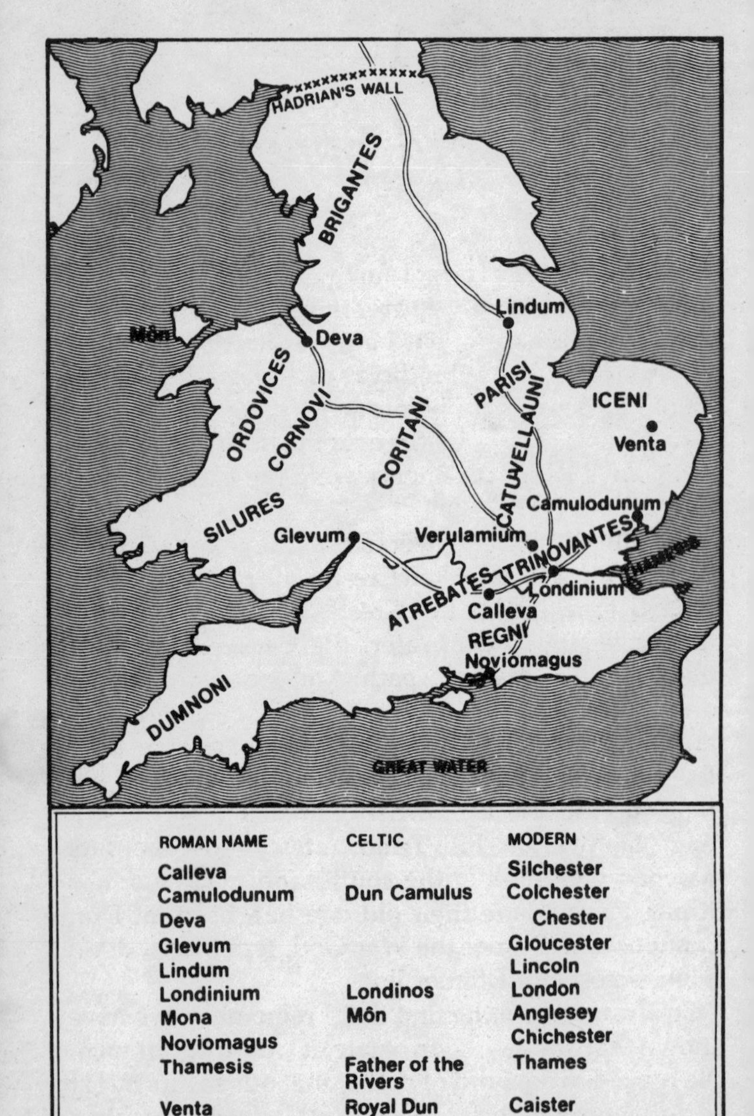

ROMAN NAME	CELTIC	MODERN
Calleva		Silchester
Camulodunum	Dun Camulus	Colchester
Deva		Chester
Glevum		Gloucester
Lindum		Lincoln
Londinium	Londinos	London
Mona	Môn	Anglesey
Noviomagus		Chichester
Thamesis	Father of the Rivers	Thames
Venta	Royal Dun	Caister
Verulamium		St. Albans

1

Sword Song

I am Cadwan of the Harp. I am the Singer of Songs and the Teller of Tales. There are, there were, many harpers among the Iceni; but I am Harper to the Queen herself; to the Lady Boudicca, as I was when I was young, to her mother before her.

That was long ago, before ever the Red Crests came, in the days when the enemy were the Catuvellauni, the Cats of War.

Five lifetimes ago, ever since they hurled their spears against the first Red Crests who came following Julius Caesar, and the Red Crests went away again in a hurry over the Great Water, the Catuvellauni have followed the conqueror's path. And the names of their kings—Cassivellaunus, Tasciovanus, Cunobelin, have been names that women use to frighten their naughty children. Many tribes, they overcame. Less than one lifetime ago, when Cunobelin was first a king, he overran the Trinovantes whose borders marched with ours in the south, and made his new Strong Place where their old one had been, at Dun Camulus, the Dun of the War God, less than a day's riding across our frontier line.

So always, from the first that I remember, we have known that one day, soon or late, it would be our turn. We prayed to the Lord of Battle, that our spears might be stronger than the spears of the Catuvellauni when that day came. We watched our borders and built great turf banks where the fens and the forest left us open to attack; and the women added the names of Cunobelin's two sons to those they used for frightening naughty children, though they were but cubs themselves as yet. "Togodumnos will catch you!" they said, and "If you do that again, Caratacus will creep in and snatch you out of your beds one dark night!"

And always, there was un-quiet along our borders; a small flurrying warfare of slave and cattle raiding at the full of the moon.

A day in hawthorn time came when the Lady Boudicca was six years old, and the King her father had moved down to his summer steading with all his household, as he often did at that time of year, to see how the foals on the southern runs were shaping. And in the lag end of the night, a man on a sweating horse brought word of raiders within our borders, loose in the grazing land between the forest and the fens. Then the King and his sword-companions came out from sleep, calling for spears and horses, and there were flaring torches and the trampling of war-ponies brought from the stables, and a yelping of horns to summon the fighting men from round about, just as I had known it all a score and a score of times before.

But after all was quiet again, when the King and his war-band were away in a green dawn with the marsh birds calling, and the hawthorn blossom showing curd pale in the darkness of the hedge around the Royal Garth, it was found that the Lady Boudicca was not in her bed in the women's quarters.

Then there began to be another kind of uproar. Maybe there would have been less if the Queen her mother had been yet alive. But Rhun, her nurse, was ever like a hen with one chick and a hawk hovering over; a thing I have noticed more than once among women who rear a child some other woman bore, and have no child of their own. And soon, all the women of the household were in full cry, scurrying here and there, crying and calling, "Boudicca! Boudicca! – Stop hiding, I can see you! – Come out from there, child of blackness! – Where are you, little bird?" And the slaves were sent flying to look in this place and that, in the foaling pens, along the fringes of the oak woods, in every pool of marsh water lest she be lying drowned among the reeds.

I knew better than that. I hitched up my harp in its embroidered mare's-skin bag – no harper worth the name is willingly parted from his harp, nor leaves her unguarded where even a friendly hand may come too near – and I set off along the way that the King and his companions had followed.

The way ran along the rich grazing country between the wide salt marshes, and the tawny wind-shaped oak woods that are the outriders of the dark forest inland. Three times I asked horse herdsmen if they had seen a girl-child go by; and the first two had seen no one since the war-band passed in the dawn: but the third man said, "A while back. She was dripping with mud and water as though she had fallen into a stream."

"And you did not think to stop her?" I said.

He scratched one ear. "Na. She would be from one of the villages round, I thought. She seemed to know where she was going, well enough."

"That would be her," I said, and pressed on.

There are many winding waters, poplar and willow fringed, among the horse-runs, and soon the way would turn inland; and I did not care to think of her once she came among the trees. The forest is good for a hunting party that knows its way, but not for one small girl-child alone. So I pushed on as fast as might be. But I had to stop and search as I went, and the sun was far to the west of noon, when I found her at last, not far short of the forest verge. She was sitting among the roots of an ancient willow tree beside one of the slow-flowing streams that vein and dapple all this countryside with winding brightness and sky-reflecting pools. And she forlorn as a fledgeling thrush new-fallen from the nest.

She had walked until she could walk no more. There was blood on one of her feet, and her hair was matted with mud; and the mud had dried into a mask on her face, save where the tracks of tears cut through it. At first I thought that she was asleep; but when I drew near, she turned, showing her teeth like a small wild thing at the nearing of danger. Then, seeing that it was I, she loosened with a little sigh; and squatting down beside her, I saw that the tear tracks were still wet.

"This is a long way that you are from home," I said, "and you with a cut foot."

And she said, "They would not take me. Still my father says I am too young. I thought maybe they would take me this time – now that I am nearly seven."

"And so you followed them."

"I thought if I followed them all the way, they would not send me back alone."

"But they rode swift as the wind on their war-ponies, and you have walked the soles off your feet," I said. "And one of them is cut and bleeding. So we will bathe it here in the stream, and then we will go home for this time. Truly the world is full of sorrow."

She tipped up her head and looked at me, proud as

any brave in his first warpaint, and let another tear run into her mouth rather than wipe it away.

"I am not crying," she said.

"Surely you are not crying. It is just the wind that has got into your eyes."

"I never cry. I am the Royal Daughter of the Iceni, and one day I shall be Queen!"

I lifted her down the bank, where the sun-streaks dappled through the willow leaves, and began to bathe her foot. "I shall hurt you," I said, "but you will not be minding that."

She shook her head; and looking up, I saw that her grief was grown smaller: a little.

"Now we will go home. See, I will carry you; and I will make you a song to shorten the way."

"Make me a sword," she said. "Old Nurse made me a sword out of two sticks, but she bound it together with wool, and it broke. Make me a sword, and then we will go home."

I thought of the hunting and calling that would still be going on, and the rings of search spreading wider and wider. And I was thinking it would do small harm to let them spread a little wider yet. It would not take long. I have always been a man of my hands, as well as a harper. I made her a sword of a thick white willow rod split with my dagger, with a short piece laid cross-wise to give it shoulders and mark off the hilt from the blade. But with what should I bind it? It must not break as Rhun's had done. I pulled round the harp-bag from my shoulder and drew out a spare harpstring of red horsehair, the thickest string that yields the deepest note. Good harpstrings are not easily come by; but it was passably strong. She was watching me, her chin almost resting on my arm, as I cut the length I needed. "See," I said, "I am binding your sword with harp-song, so that it will never break. Let you give me three hairs from your head to use also, that it may be like your father's great sword that has goldwork in the hilt."

She pulled me out three hairs and gave them to me, and I dipped them in the water to rid them of mud, and twisted them together with the harpstring, and bound her sword, and gave it to her.

She looked at it, and sighed. She had known that it could be only a toy sword made of willow wood; but her heart had hoped for something more. "One day I shall have a real sword," she said; and then, "You could make me a real song, now."

She was growing a little sleepy, even then.

"Surely I will make you a real song," I told her, and picked her up, muffling my cloak about her, for a small mean wind was blowing up off the marshes, and a silvery haze dimming the westering sun. And I set out, back the way that we had come. "I will make you the song I promised you for home-going. And one day, when you have a great sword like the King your father's, I will make you a great song of the Victories of a Queen. But now, I will make you only a little song, to match with your little sword."

And I sang to her as we went along, taking the words as they came into my head:

> "Listen now, for your sword is singing,
> 'I am the proud one, I that am sword to a Queen.
> The sun flames not more brightly than my hilt,
> The night cannot outshine my blade's dark sheen.
> The earth shall tremble at our passing;
> We will make the warhosts scatter, she and I.'

But now the light fades
And the wild duck home are winging,
And sleep falls like dew from the quiet sky.
'Sleep now,' says your sword,
'Sleep now, you and I.'"

By the time I had done, her head was growing heavy in the hollow of my shoulder.

So I carried her home to the household that was like a disturbed ants' nest in the dusk, more than any other thing that I can call to mind. Rhun the Nurse came running to meet me with a white face that looked as though she had not slept for a hundred years. And I put Boudicca into her arms, still in her sleep holding to the play-thing sword that I had made for her.

"Here she is," I said, "she had followed the war-band. Take better care of her another time."

2

A Colt for the Breaking

I have not forgotten, in more than five and twenty summers. I have not forgotten, the great Song of a Queen's Victories that I promised to the Princess Boudicca.

It is all here, garnered within me, the things that should go to the making of such a song; the things that I have known with my own eyes and ears, the things that have come to me through the eyes and ears of others, the things that my own heart within me tells me must have been in this way or that way. All the things that make up the life pattern, the life song, of Boudicca the Queen of the Iceni.

How should I begin my song?

I would sing first of the King's high Hall in the midst of the Royal Dun, the fires burning always down its length, and the paved space between the fires, where the women made the Corn Dance at harvest time. And the warriors gathered to the evening feasting, with their weapons laid behind them. And the skulls of ancient enemies daubed with red and yellow ochre, grinning along the great tie-beams where the firelight scarcely reached; and the laughter, and the harp-notes flying like sparks from the fire in windy weather. And the women's quarters ranged behind the Hall, where the women wove scarlet and purple on the standing loom, or sent for me to come and play to them while they sat combing their hair; and where, in the Royal

Chamber, on the bedplace piled with goose-feather pillows of embroidered green and crimson and blue, on a night that smelled outside of grass and elder-flowers and thunder brewing over the marshes, my Lady Boudicca was born.

I heard her first cry, squatting in the little side door-way that gave out into the chariot court, with my harp silent across my knees. And a woman of the Kindred came to me and said, "Still there, Watchdog? The Queen has borne a Royal Daughter to her Lord, and so the line goes on." For we are an old People, and among us the Kingship goes not from father to son, but down the Moonside, the Womanside; and the King becomes King only because his sword is strong and he is wedded to the Queen.

So I was the first to know, even before the Priest Kind sounded the moon call on the sacred oxhorns, that was taken up and sent on and on from end to end of the land, telling the People of the Horse that a new Royal Daughter was born to carry forward the life of the tribe.

And I took my harp and went and walked a while among the half-tamed trees of the apple garth, making a small music just between myself and the stars.

I would sing of the horse herds grazing in the broad pastures between the forest and the fen lands; the proud-necked stallions and the leggy two-year-olds and the trained chariot teams and the mares in foal. And the wide-winged sunsets over the marshes, caught and flung back by the reedy lakes and winding waterways until it seems as though earth as well as sky is turned to fire. I would sing of wild geese flighting down from the north in the autumn nights, and the thick green-smelling darkness of the forest verges in high summer when the cuckoo's voice is breaking; and the swirling pattern, red-enamelled on the bronze face of the King's warshield, that I have seen her tracing with one finger, as though she would find some secret in it.

I would sing of all these things, for it seems to me that all these things gave something of themselves to the making of the Lady Boudicca.

When she was four years old, her mother went beyond the sunset, taking with her the seven-month man-child who had never drawn breath in this world. So I would sing of the death-fires for a Queen; and how, after they were cold, the People of the Horse had no Queen anymore, but a Royal Daughter who carried the Queenship within her, as seed time carries harvest, for a future day.

Four is over young for long grieving, so when the Lady Boudicca had wept a while, she grew happy again, trotting like a hound pup at her father's heels whenever she could escape from the women's side, save for the times when she came trotting at mine.

The years went by, and the years went by, and the wild geese came flighting down the autumn gales, and the mares dropped their foals in early summer. And still we looked to our southern and our western borders, and felt to be sure that our swords sat loosely in the sheath.

And the year came when Boudicca was thirteen summers old, and it was time for choosing who should be her Marriage Lord and take up the old King's sword when he must lay it down. Then, when the harvest was over, the King called out the Oak Priests from their sacred clearings in the forest, and summoned the chiefs and nobles of the tribe to the Choosing Feast. Chiefs of the Parisi, too, the chariot warriors who had spread along the coasts to our north and become bound to us by blood ties so that now we counted almost as one people. Almost, but not quite.

The chiefs and the nobles gathered. Too many for the guest-huts, too many to crowd within the Hall, and so the black horsehide tents were pitched in the in-pasture below the Royal Village, and the great fires were made in the King's forecourt. The Weapon Court, we called it, from the tall black stone that stood there for the warriors to sharpen their weapons on in time of war. And for three days and far into three nights the feasting went on, and the King and the chiefs and the Priest Kind took council together, while the Princess Boudicca and the women of the Kindred remained shut away in the women's quarters.

And on the first morning of the Choosing Feast, the King sacrificed a young black stallion to Epona the Lady of the Horse Herds, the All Mother without whom there can be neither children to the tribe nor foals to the herds nor barley to the fields. And on the first night of the Choosing Feast, the freshly flayed hide was laid out in the midst of the apple garth, and Merddyn, chief of the Oak Priests, lay down upon it to sleep the Choosing Sleep, that Epona might come to him in his dreaming, and give him of her wisdom to carry back with him to the Council Fire.

And on the third evening of the Feast, the Choosing was finished; and after, as it seemed to me, the choice had hovered around half the young braves of the tribe, it fell at last upon one, Prasutagus, son of Dumnorix, who was of the Iceni on his mother's side, but his father a chieftain of the Parisi.

It had taken the full three days to make the Choosing; and even after it was made, there were growlings and murmurings, for never before had we followed a King who was not pure bred to the Horse People; and not all men thought well of the new way of things.

Not all women either.

In the noontide after the Choosing Feast was ended and the chiefs and nobles had gone their ways, I was walking to and fro in the apple garth, for there was a new song on me, and at such times I need always to walk. And Boudicca came up through the old wind-shaped trees, with her skirts kilted through her belt, and a pair of throw-spears in her hand, just as she must have come from the practice ground. We are not like some tribes whose women go to war with the men in the usual pattern of things, only in times of sorest need our women follow the war-trail with us and we lead our mares under the chariot yoke; yet our mares are broken to harness and our women learn to use their spears, lest the need be upon us.

"I heard your harp," she said, "and so I came."

I had no need to ask her why. Ever since the day of the willow-wood sword she had come to me in time of trouble, before ever she would go to Rhun her nurse.

There was an old tree at the head of the garth, half-fallen into the grass, but with its little hard apples already russet-gold among its grey wind-bitten leaves. She sat herself down on the sloping trunk, and I settled in the long grass at her feet, and looked up at her, waiting for her to tell me what she would be telling me, in her own good time.

And because of the Choosing Feast, all at once I saw her with a freshly opened eye, and knew with a small ache of loss, that it was not a child I looked at anymore, despite the small white scar on her temple where she had fallen out of a tree when she was ten. She was tall; taller than many boys of her age; and held herself that day like a Queen, her head braced upright as though already it carried the weight of the moon headdress. Her mane of strong straight hair sprang from her head as though with a life of its own, yellow as autumn birch leaves. Soon now, I thought, she would have to braid it after the manner of the Women's side. Her eyes under their winged and feathery golden brows seemed darker than their usual blue, as the saltmarsh darkens when a cloud shadow passes over. I had seen them darkened like that before; I had seen her in a rage often enough; it had never lasted, and ended as like as not in laughter. But looking up at her now, I saw that this was something else than rage, and would not end so soon nor so easily. And I hoped in my heart that the Lord Prasutagus would know how to handle it, for assuredly no one else could.

She sat so long, the spears in the crook of her arm, looking down between the apple trees, that I began to think she had forgotten I was there. Then she said, "They have sent for Prasutagus, already."

"They would be doing that," I said. "As soon as the Choosing was over."

"Why should they be in so great a hurry? There is time enough."

"He is an unbroken colt – like the colts that our horse-masters break in to harness in their second winter. He must be broken in to the Kingship, and in this world, who can be sure how much or how little there is of time."

"There is time enough," she said again, as though clinging to the words for a talisman – or a weapon. "I hate them all! The King my father is still young and his sword-arm strong."

It was in my mind to say "Surely. And tomorrow he may ride hunting and come home on a hurdle." But instead, I said, "This Prasutagus is seventeen, already two years past his manhood-making. If he is to be trained to a new life, the sooner it is done the better. Let you remember it will be no easy thing for him; no easier than for the two-year-olds when they are brought in off the freedom of the far-runs and trained to run under the chariot yoke."

"Why should it be easy for him?" she demanded. "It will not be easy for me, to be mated to a man I have never seen before."

"You will have come to know him well enough, long before the women make the Bride Song for you."

But she was not listening. "Why should it be a stranger, and not Vadrex or Cassal?"

"Does your heart go out to Vadrex or Cassal? I have heard you say that Vadrex has only spots where his beard should be."

She laughed at that. But the laughter cracked in her throat. "Na," she said, after a moment. "But at least they are not strangers. Why must they choose a man out of the Parisi?"

"You ask so many questions, my head goes round," I said, trying to keep the thing light. "The Parisi are great warriors."

"So are we."

"And so are the Catuvellauni who press ever closer along our borders. It may be that a day comes when it will be well for the Iceni that the Parisi are bonded to them by marriage with the Royal Daughter – with the Queen."

She was silent again, a long time. Then she said in a small breathless voice, "One day I must take a Marriage Lord, that there may be a chief to lead the tribe in war, and another Royal Daughter to carry forward unbroken the Life Line of the People. But not yet. I would not take him yet. I would take my sword under the covers with me at night, as the young braves do, and have my freedom still. And if the Catuvellauni come against us, and – and my father is not here to lead the War Host, I would lead them myself. It would not be the first time that the People of the Horse have followed a woman on the war-trail – and she not needing any prince of the Parisi to bear her weapons for her."

And then at last, she brought her gaze back from the distance between the apple trees, and looked down at me. "Cadwan of the Harp, do you remember how once you promised me I should have a great sword like my father's, and you would make me a great song of a Queen's Victories?"

"I remember," I said, "and then I made you a toy sword of white willow wood, and a small foolish song to go with it."

"I have the sword still, and the song. Do you mind how often I begged it of you when I was a child – long after I had it by heart. But still, I would be having the great song you promised me, one day."

"One day," I said.

"And the sword, too."

A little chill wind came up through the long grass, and for a moment it was as though a shadow passed between us and the sun.

3

The Bride Cup

Five days later the Lord Prasutagus drove into the Royal Dun.

The watchers on the gateway saw his dustcloud on the track from the north-west, and at the heart of the dustcloud a seed of dark that grew and flowered into a chariot drawn by a four-horse team in the Roman manner. He had been driving at full gallop on the last stretch, far out-distancing his companions and the pack beasts that followed behind. But at the foot of the slope where the track begins to climb through the Royal Village, he reined back, and came in through the gate at last, not in a thunder of hooves and iron-shod wheels and spun clods, as most young men would have done, for the show of the thing, but at a gentler and more courteous pace.

He held the reins himself, though his charioteer stood beside him – I came to know him later for a man who liked best to be his own driver, which sometimes his charioteers found hard to bear – and for sure he handled the dun team as well as ever a man could do.

Beside the weapon-stone he brought them to a halt, tossed the reins to the charioteer, and sprang down before the wheels had ceased to turn, and came on towards where the King waited for him in the doorway of the Hall. And as he came, a pair of brindled wolfhounds, the finest that ever I had seen, came bounding from behind the chariot, to follow at his heels.

And so we took our first look, all of us gathered there, at Prasutagus of the Parisi, who was chosen to be Boudicca's Marriage Lord and our next King.

He was short, but strongly framed, and his shoulders under his blue and russet cloak had broadened before the usual time, so that at seventeen he was already built like a man. His hair was darkly and fiercely red, with the same metallic golden glint at the ends that a bay horse shows in the sunlight; and under it, his eyes were sombre, but his mouth wide and, I judged, well used to laughter. He had a fighter's face, but a thinker's also; he would be a hard councillor as well as a warrior, by and by. "The gods grant," I thought, "that his council be good."

He came up to the King, and gave him the spear-salute.

"You sent for me, my Lord the King, and I am come."

"Welcome is your coming," said the King. "You know for what purpose you are called?"

"I know for what purpose I am called."

"And are you willing in your heart to answer the Call, and to follow the way that lies before you?"

I wondered how many times those ritual questions had been asked and answered since first the Iceni were a People. And suddenly I wondered what the Priest Kind would do to any man who, having once been Chosen, refused the Call. It was a foolish thought. The sun does not take a whim to rise in the west. The pattern of things is the pattern of things.

Prasutagus said, "In my heart, I am willing."

But his voice had quickened, and he said it, not as

one making the ritual answer, but as one speaking his own mind; and his eyes had gone past the King, to where Boudicca came out from among the maidens in her father's Hall, bearing the Guest Cup in her hands.

And truly, she was worth the looking at; a figure all of gold, in her best gown of saffron wool, her hair braided and shining, the gold torque of the Royal Daughter circling her long neck. "Drink," she said, "and be welcome."

But she made it very clear that her words were the ritual ones, and nothing more.

He took the cup from her and drank. They looked at each other across the rim, their eyes nearly on a level. I have said that she was tall for her age; I have said that he was short for his; and I saw that she knew it, and was trying to make herself taller yet, and that he knew it also. There was a sudden fiery flush along his cheek-bones, as he gave the cup back into her hands.

The coming together was not going to be easy, between those two.

"But there will be time," I thought. "Time for them to grow towards each other, if the gods are kind."

There was two years of time. Two years and a little more. While still Boudicca was the Royal Daughter in the women's quarters, and Prasutagus had his place among the young braves of the household, sleeping among them in the long half-loft above the Hall at night, and learning the ways of the Iceni and the ways of kingship.

And then the time for the marriage feast drew near. And Merddyn and his fellow priests traced strange patterns in red and yellow sand by day, and looked up into the wheeling stars by night, and chose a day not long before Samhein, the feast of in-gathering when the flocks and herds are gathered in from the far grazing-runs and folded close against the winter storms, and when the souls of the dead also come homing to their own firesides.

Then, as always when a great marriage feast is in the wind, there began to be a constant coming and going of merchants and swordsmiths and workers in precious stones. For the King must give fine new weapons to the man who wed his daughter; and Prasutagus must choose out three bride gifts for his wedding night, according to the custom. There was much whispering among the women as to what those would be; for Prasutagus's father was among the richest of the chiefs of the Parisi, and his gifts would be worth the having.

But less than half a moon before the appointed day, word came of a raiding party of the Catuvellauni laying waste our borders to the south-west. It was word that came often enough, but this was a greater war-band than the usual run of such things, and pressing far in along the High Chalk that makes a ridgeway linking us to the outside world. Always the traders have come and gone along that way, and our horses have followed it to the markets of the south and west; always it has been our place of greatest danger from attack, and we have kept the turf walls up and the guard bands alert, so that few raiders came that way. But this was no cattle raid half in sport. This was a strong war-company, leaving a trail of burned-out steadings behind them, and driving off all living things that came their way.

And again, the war-horns sounded to call in the fighting men, and the chariots were harnessed, and the King with his household warriors, Prasutagus among them, drove out to clear the borders, under a raiding moon.

They were gone seven days, and returned at the twixt-light hour when the first owls are crying and the flare of torches has begun to bite. There was a first thin crackling of ice in the chariot ruts, and the breath of the horses smoked in the air as they came up between the tall gate-stones of the Weapon Court. And there were captured horses among them, and the heads of slain raiders swinging by their long hair knotted to the chariot rails. But there were gaps in our own ranks, too, and they came without shouting or triumph. And Prasutagus drove the King's chariot; and on the chariot floor, bound down that it might not jolt out, lay the body of the King, under his shield.

In the gathering throng, the women had begun to keen: and men came running with torches, as he was lifted out and laid on the cold ground before the threshold. And then the crowd parted, and the Princess Boudicca came through. She stood long and long, looking down at her father's body; and once she swayed a little, like a lone cornstalk in a breath of wind, then steadied herself. "Bring him into his Hall," she said in a small level voice. And then she looked up and met Prasutagus's gaze; and she cried out on him, sudden and wailing, "Why must it be him instead of you?"

And Prasutagus looked back at her, with a great smear of dried blood across his cheek, and said, "Because the mark was on his forehead, not on mine."

And they bore the King into his Hall.

So the death-fires burned for the old King; and when they were cold, his ashes were laid away in the

Royal House of Sleep, with his finest spear and his great bronze-faced shield and his sword with the goldwork on the hilt, that he might be armed as befits a High Chieftain for his journey beyond the sunset. And when all was over, and the proper sacrifices made, the Oak Priests led Boudicca up to the crest of the long grave mound, where our Queens have been made since first we were a People, and showed her to the assembled chieftains on the north and the south and the east and the west; crying out to each quarter, "People of the Horse, here is your Queen to you. Do you accept her?"

And from each quarter the chieftains gave her the royal salute, their spears crashing on their shields. "We accept her, we accept her, we accept her."

And in the sight of them all, Merddyn the Chief of the Oak Priests, set on her head the tall silver head-dress of the moon. And so she became our Queen, Goddess-on-Earth to us; the Life of the Tribe in her keeping. And all the while her face was like a painted mask in the torchlight that sprang towards her up the grave mound; and her eyes in it only dark holes with the night sky showing through. And I thought, "She is too young – too young – too young. . . ."

Late, late that night, Boudicca went to the great weapon kist in the Royal Chamber, and brought out the plain long sword with the hilt of age-darkened nawhal ivory that had been her father's when he was young, before ever he came to be King. And she took it beside her into the broad rug-piled bedplace where she had never slept before.

The nine days of mourning were accomplished, and the fires that had been quenched on the hearths were kindled again. And then it was the appointed time for the Bride Feast and the making of the new King. And before the assembled chiefs and great ones of the tribe, Boudicca and Prasutagus stood together on the threshold of the Hall – all thresholds are sacred places, the royal threshold above all others – she in her mantle of curd-white mare's skin, the silver plates of the moon headdress that hung down against her cheeks catching and losing the wintry light; he in the King's great cloak of red stallion's hide. They spoke the words that Merddyn demanded of them, and held out their hands while he made the marriage cut first on her wrist and then on his, and bound them lightly together with a rawhide thong. They stood so joined while a few bright drops of mingled blood spattered down upon the threshold. Then Merddyn loosed off the binding, and another priest brought forward one of the old King's spears and touched Prasutagus with it, first on the forehead, then on the breast, then gave it into his hand. That is all the kingmaking ceremony there is, among the Horse People. Marriage to the Royal Woman, that is the real kingmaking ceremony. And so when they turned and went back together into the Hall, he was the King.

Then the cooking-pits were opened, and the feasting began. And midway through the feasting, Prasutagus brought from the breast of his tunic a necklace of amber and red cornelian and curiously twisted gold wires, shining like the sun, and put it round Boudicca's neck. And that was the first of his Bride Gifts to her. And later, his charioteer brought into the Hall a young riding mare, mealy of mane and tail, and dark golden as heather honey, so light in her moving that her hooves seemed scarcely to touch the fern-strewn floor. And that was the second of his Bride Gifts.

And all the while, I watched Boudicca; on the threshold, at the feasting, when Prasutagus hung the fiery jewels round her neck, when she reached out to touch the mare's forehead in token of acceptance. I watched her when I woke my harp and sang her the marriage song that I had made for her; – much thought and much love and much walking in the apple garth, that song had cost me – and when she stepped out with him onto the paved dancing-floor, she with a long trail of ivy in her hand, he with a barbed and whippy branch of holly, to lead the Man-and-Woman dancing. And all the while, I thought, "She is too young! Grief upon me! She is too young. They should have given her more time."

And yet I knew that with the old King dead, there was no more time to give.

Far on into the night Boudicca and her Marriage Lord went together to the Royal Chamber. I mind he held out his hand to her. But she walked beside him not touching it. In the doorway the women threw corn over their heads to bring them many children; a golden shower in the light of the spitting pine-knot torches. And there was laughing and jostling, and as many as the chamber would hold thrust in after them while the rest hung about the doorway.

In the heart of the chamber, the bedplace was piled deep with fine wolf and deerskin rugs against the icy draughts that whistled along the floor; for the wind was rising, and would be blowing a full gale from off the sea by dawn. And standing at the foot of the bedplace, the women took the silver moon headdress from Boudicca, and stripped her naked, then flung a cloak round her against the cold; while the young braves did the same for Prasutagus the King. And then it was time for the last ceremony of all. For drinking the Bride Cup of apple wine and honey and certain herbs. And Boudicca looked to her women, for Rhun to bring it to her. But before the old nurse could make any move, Prasutagus crooked a finger to Cadog, his armour-bearer, and the boy stepped out from the shadows, bearing a cup that was certainly no Bride Cup of the Iceni. A cup such as I had never seen before; and strange, very strange.

It was a glass calyx, I judged of Roman workmanship; but I had seen Roman glass before, none like this; an inner cup held within an outer; yet the outer was indeed no cup at all, but an interweaving tangle of figures that seemed to stand clear away from the glass behind them. Later, when I came to know it well, and had more than once held it in my hands, I knew that the figures were strange indeed; half-man and half-horse, with struggling girls caught among them, and all linked and laced together with the twisted branches of trees, and that they touched the inner calyx nowhere but at the rim and the base. Surely, even among the Romans, there must be some who have the secret of magic-making. That night, I knew only that it was strange and beautiful, and that it was green. The dark, lifeless and lightless green of forest depths in late summer.

Prasutagus took it from his armour-bearer, and held it to Boudicca. She looked, but made no move to take it. "What is this?"

"Your Bride Cup," he said.

"It is no cup of mine."

"It is now," Prasutagus said in his level voice. "It is my third Bride Gift to you."

And his voice was gentle, but the set of his mouth

was that of a man who will wait a very long time, but will not in the end be denied.

There was silence. No more laughter in the Royal Chamber, only the soughing of the rising wind across the thatch, and somewhere the mocking cry of an owl. And in the heart of the silence, I watched the battle of wills between those two. And I knew what it meant to Prasutagus that she should drink the Bride wine from that cup of his giving. She was among her own kind in her own world; he was the stranger, coming in from outside. For two years he had been broken and trained like a chariot pony, and had not found it easy, even as I had said to Boudicca in the apple garth. He was nothing in his own right, only because he had been chosen to marry with the Queen. He was young and proud, and to make the matter worse for him, he loved her. Therefore he had given her this third gift; the most beautiful thing that he could find, a lover's gift; therefore he was determined that she should drink the Bride drink from it. In this one thing he would be her Marriage Lord indeed.

At last, Boudicca gave a little sigh, and put out her hands to take the cup. She held it so lightly, looking down into it, that for a moment I wondered if she were going to deliberately part her hands and let it fall and shatter on the flagged floor. But she raised it and drank. And as she did so, the full magic of the cup appeared; for as the light of the pine-knot torches caught and shone through it, it flamed from its dark shadow-green into shadowy fires, glowing with the furnace colours of a winter sunset over the marsh. There was a murmur, a breath of startled wonder, from those of us looking on. But Boudicca made no sign, only drank, and gave the cup again to Prasutagus. His hand enclosed hers for an instant as he took it back; then he drained the cup and turned to give it to Old Nurse, who was hovering near. And again, now that it had lost the torchlight, it had returned to its dust-dark forest green.

Then as the women pulled back the heavy bed-rugs, Boudicca went to her clothes' kist, and took up from it and unsheathed the old King's sword. Some of the men drew a whistling breath through the teeth, but I am thinking that the women knew already what was coming now. She knelt beside the great bedplace and leaned far over, to lay the naked blade down the centre of it. I mind how the torchlight played with the grey burnished iron.

Boudicca came back to her feet, and stood looking at her red-haired Marriage Lord.

"My Lord Prasutagus, over there is your sleeping place, and over here is mine. Let you bide on your own side under your own cloak, until maybe I bid you come closer."

And he stood looking back at her, rocking gently, with his hands on his hips, and the corners of his wide mouth twitching into laughter. "No hurry," he said. "Boudicca, Honey-sweet, you are not the first girl that was ever under my cloak; but I never yet had a girl that did not come warm and willing; and I'll not begin with my own Queen."

4

The Sword on the Threshold

Late into the next spring, when the swallows were at their nesting under the thatch, the thing happened that changed all the world

The Red Crests came again.

Word of their coming reached us along the trade routes in the usual way of things; and suddenly the Catuvellauni were gone from our borders, as King Togodumnos gathered his War Host and swept south to meet them. There was a great battle, and the Catuvellauni were driven back to the Father of Rivers, and another battle for the ford above the trading post of Londinos and again the Catuvellauni were forced back, and Togodumnos was slain, so that Caratacus his younger brother was after that the lone leader of the War Host.

A strange thing it must have seemed to the Cats of War, to be driven back in defeat; they who for so long had trodden the conqueror's path.

Then the chieftains and nobles and the mightiest warriors of the Iceni gathered to the Council Fire, and some among the young men, the hot-headed and hot-hearted, were for over-running the lands of the Catuvellauni while their spears were busy elsewhere; and some were for joining them to hurl the Red Crests back into the sea.

But for the most part, the chiefs and the older men were of another way of thinking. And Gretorix Hard-Council stood up before the rest, twisting the ends of his badger-streaked beard round his fingers in the way that he had, and said, "If we swarm into the Catuvellauni's hunting runs, and their spears prevail against the Red Crests, then we shall have them to answer to afterwards, and they will still be a Tribe many times greater than we. And if the Red Crests prevail, then we shall have gained nothing, and may have lost much. If we join spears with the Catuvellauni to drive the Red Crests out, then we shall still have the Catuvellauni on our frontiers afterwards; and if it is we that are driven back, then we shall join them under the Red Crests' heel. And why should we risk that, we who owe nothing to the Cats of War? My counsel is that we bide quiet by our own hearths. And if the Catuvellauni have the victory, then at least the gaining of it may weaken them for a life-time or so, and we shall have lost nothing. And if it is the Red Crests who have the victory, then let us seek to make an alliance with them – so we may not stand alone against the War Cats in years to come."

Then there was much talk and argument round the Council Fire. Hot hearts against cool heads; until it came to the time for the Queen to speak. And she rose from her High Seat of piled bulls' hides, and stood before all her chiefs and elders. And the silence was so great it seemed to me I could hear the air passing through my harpstrings. She was very white, and her eyes darkened as I had seen them do before; and said, looking round at them all, "Gretorix Hard-Council has said that we owe nothing to the Cats of War. That is not a true word. We owe them the death of the King my father. Let us bide by our own hearths, and let them rot beneath the Red Crests' heel!"

I thought, "What a woman's way, what a vixen's way, to set the fate of two tribes and maybe many more, over against the death of one man!" And I looked at Prasutagus sitting beside her with his sword across his knees, and saw the thought in him also – and in Gretorix Hard-Council and others about the fire. And then I saw the face of Merddyn Oak Priest, his dark gaze turned upon her, and the shadow of a smile on his thin lips; and I knew that it was the Priest Kind, before ever the Council Fire was lit, who had put that way of thinking into her heart. That seemed to me an ill thing. Yet the ruling, which in its way bore out the words of Gretorix Hard-Council, seemed to me good; though it was not the kind that great songs are made of.

So the thing was settled, and Prasutagus's hand fell gently away from the hilt of his sword.

And we bided quiet by our hearths for that time.

We waited, while the Catuvellauni lay up in the refuge of the forest country north of Londinos; they and the Red Crests watching each other like beasts over a kill. And then in high summer, we heard that the Emperor of the Roman people had come himself, and with him many more Red Crests, and magic war-animals, many times bigger than the biggest horse that was ever foaled, whose voice was the bellowing of many war-horns, whose hide was tough enough to turn a spear, and who made the earth to shudder when they charged, scattering and trampling on all that came their way.

Then there was a battle greater than any that had gone before, and the Catuvellauni were hacked to pieces; and Caratacus escaped with nothing but his life and a handful of his sword-companions, and fled to take up arms again, with the Silures of the western hills.

And then there was quiet. And in the quiet, word came that the Emperor had taken Dun Camulus without a blow, and sat himself down there to receive the surrender of the Catuvellauni. And while he was there, other Kings began going to him under the Green Branch, seeking a good peace. Then the Iceni held council again, and determined upon following the same trail. And at that Council it was also decided that, both because the Romans were not used to Woman's rule and might not understand, and because it might be a trap to get the rulers of the tribes into their hands, Prasutagus alone, with a company of chiefs and elders, should go to the gathering at Dun Camulus, while Boudicca bided safe in the heart of her people.

She raged at this. Half, I expected her to follow until her feet were bleeding, as she had done that time before. But even for Boudicca there could be no going against the whole Council when its word was spoken.

I rode south with Prasutagus, for at all the great happenings of a tribe, the Chief's Harper must be there to make of it a harp-song that may pass into the history of that tribe.

So we drove south, between the marsh and the upland forests with the cornlands ripening to the harvest, and the dustclouds of late summer rising from the horses' hooves and the chariot wheels. And I saw the great Dun of the Catuvellauni, with the King's palace in its midst, many times larger and finer than the Royal Dun of the Iceni; and set about with its wide forecourts and chariot courts, its craftsmen's quarter and its Women's Place. And I saw the Emperor of the Romans sitting in the High Hall of Togodumnos. Claudius, they called him. He was a sight to make a cat laugh in his gilded armour (but the Cats of War would not be laughing anymore). A man with a big paunch and a little head on a long neck, who stammered like a midsummer cuckoo in his speech, and limped when I saw him walking. He seemed well pleased with all things, himself included. And yet I saw that like young Prasutagus, he had a thinking face. And so far as might be, across the gulf between us, I warmed to the man.

There were as many Kings gathered there as there are fingers on my two hands, counting the small with the great. And each had a man, most often a merchant, to stand beside him and the Emperor when they spoke together, and turn their spoken words to and fro, from the tongue of the tribes to the tongue of Rome and back again. Only one or two of those from the south, where there had been coming and going for many years between themselves and Rome, could speak the Roman tongue, and carried themselves tall, accordingly. Cogidubnos of the Regni was chief among them, having been almost a Roman princeling before ever the Red Crests came. It is in my mind that if he had chosen, Prasutagus could have been another, for the Parisi have ever been strongly linked with Gaul, and in Gaul all men speak the Roman tongue. But he was there to speak for the Iceni, and he had his merchant to stand beside him like the rest.

Three days we remained in Dun Camulus – Camulodunum, the Red Crests had begun to call it, in their own tongue. And I saw the great war-beasts that

Claudius had brought with him. Elephants, they are called; and they are not magic, only strange to us. Mighty indeed are those beasts, and their drivers sit astride their necks behind their great flapping ears; and on their backs in battle they carry things like wheel-less chariots in which archers and javelin men ride. Yet out of battle they are oddly gentle, and if their driver lies down in front of them, they will feel for him as delicately as a maiden picking flowers, with the tip of the long waving thing that grows from their heads where their muzzles should be, and step over him not harming a hair of his head. And I have heard it said that their great hearts fail with fear at the barking of a little dog. Sad it is for the Catuvellauni that they did not know that thing.

So the days of the great Council went by, with feasting at each day's end; and the Kings and chiefs made their peace and swore alliance with Rome.

And then we took the road north again.

Boudicca stood in the gateway of the Weapon Court to greet her Lord. "Are we a free people yet?" she asked, as he reined in and dropped from his chariot.

He said, "While we pay a yearly tribute of gold and horses and young men to serve beside the Red Crests."

"Then we are not a free people."

"We are what the Emperor and his Ministers call a free state. Gretorix Hard-Council will tell you what that means; and Cadwan of the Harp will make you a harp-song of the splendours that we have seen in Caesar's camp. I am very tired, my Queen."

The Emperor Claudius went back to Rome at summer's end, leaving behind him orders for Dun

Camulus to be rebuilt as a Roman city, and giving it all the special rights of a colony, a place for his Red Crests to settle on the land when their years with the Eagles were over. Leaving also men to see that the work was done.

But up in the horse country, we had other things to think of; for with the harvest over it was time to be rounding up the herds, and cutting out the yearlings for branding and the half-wild two-year-olds to be run up to the corrals for breaking and making.

And on a day of soft fitful wind and the changing lights of early autumn weather, Boudicca and Prasutagus with some of the companions rode out to see the first of the herds brought in from the upland pastures. The thunder that had been muttering low over the marshes all day, had begun to circle to the south, where the land was shadowed under banks of flat-topped anvil-cloud. And as we came down towards the place where the oak scrub fell back, and the droveway broadened and ran out into open pasture, there came a flick of lightning bright enough to make a blink in the daylight, and then from above the woods inland, a whip-crack of thunder that boomed and rumbled away hollow over the marshes towards the sea.

We were riding well strung out, and, not aware of it, I had drawn some way ahead of the rest. My horse, who was young and nervous, began to dance and sweat, and I reined him aside into the woodshore tangle of goat sallow and brambles and tall-growing marsh ragwort as I heard the others coming up behind me. Prasutagus and my Lady Boudicca passed close by me; and it seemed that there was war between them – there was often war between them at that time, the attacking for the most part on her side – for her colour was up and her eyes overbright, and as they reined in just ahead of me, looking out over the open valley and the droveway, he was saying in the tone of a man goaded to the quick, "Do you think that it was joy to me to kneel before the Emperor of Rome, and swear faith to him? I carried out the Council's orders – which were your orders above all, my Queen. If the thing seems ill to you, now that it is done, let you speak of it to Gretorix and the greybeards, and do not come laying the thing at my threshold!"

Far up the droveway, where it curved from sight among the oak woods, I thought I heard something: a flurry of shouting; but the soft gusts blew the sound away.

"Had you no voice of your own at the Council Fire, then?" Boudicca flung at him over her shoulder. "You are the King, do you count for nothing?"

Aiee! The unreason of women!

They must have known that I was there, but truly I think they did not care.

Prasutagus took a deep, slow breath. "We all know how much the King counts for among the Horse People until he has proved himself a War leader; until he has given daughters and sons to the Queen." But he did not give his anger free rein even then, but spoke steadily and with hard-held patience. "You know what chance I have had to prove my spear hand; and for the rest – Boudicca, I have kept my promise to you, and your father's sword yet lies between us."

And in my heart I cried out to him "Listen now! the time for patience begins to be over! The time comes when pride will not let her set that sword aside, even though she long to do it, if nothing comes to force her hand!"

Then as the rest came up, she struck away his hand that was resting lightly on her bridle, and drove her heels into her mare's flanks and broke forward and down towards the droveway.

And then – it seemed as though all things happened at once, with no before or after, no order to their happening. The light was going as the storm clouds spread up against the sky, and there came another blink of lightning and a thunder crack almost upon us; and round the curve of the droveway and spreading out over the open ground, came the herd, like a dark river in spate. They ran wildly, terrified, stampeding as driven beasts will from what would have done little more than startle them if they had been at graze. They were almost upon Boudicca as she saw the danger and wrenched her mare round. The turf was slippery from the long dry summer, and – there was no time to see how it came about – the mare lost her hind legs and went half down; and the Queen was lying against the rotten trunk of an alder tree long since fallen into the grass beside the way, while the poor beast, with a shriek of terror, gathered her legs under her again and fled on from the dark flood of her own kind.

We were all out from the woodshore and racing headlong for the same spot, though indeed there was little enough we could do, no more than the yelling herdsmen hurling their beasts along the flanks of the stampede. Prasutagus was out ahead, having gone after Boudicca almost in the moment that she broke away. He reached her as the forerunners of the herd were upon her; no time to catch her up and get clear. He dropped from his own horse in full career, and flung himself upon her, forcing her in against the alder trunk, and shielding her body with his own, as the flood of hooves poured over them.

That much I saw, even as I was caught up in the force of the stampede and whirled away. For a while, long or short, I would not be knowing, it was all that I could do to keep my own horse from going down; then I got him round and began to force him back against the flood. Upreared heads and thrusting shoulders were all about me, wild eyes and flaring nostrils and streaming manes. But the press was thinning. The dustcloud was sinking, and there was clear ground round the alder trunk when I got back to it; and men swinging down from their horses, and the Queen on her feet again, standing by; and all looking down at the Lord Prasutagus lying still on the trampled ground.

Sure I am that but for the little shelter of that half-rotten tree trunk, they must both have died. As it was – well, the Queen was seemingly unharmed. They had turned the boy over in lifting him off her; and he lay with his face tipped up to the first heavy drops of thunder rain. A little blood ran from the corner of his mouth and more out of his hair above one ear; and his tunic, half-torn from his body, showed the flesh of his flanks and shoulders bruised and broken.

After the tumult and thunder of hooves, the shouting men and screaming of horses, it was very still.

Boudicca asked, "Is he dead?" Her face was as grey-white as his own; and then she said, so quietly that I think I who was standing nearest to her must have been the only one who heard, "Let him not be dead!"

"He is not dead," someone said, "but his spirit is out of his body for this while."

Boudicca drew in a quick breath, "Let someone ride back for a Healer Priest to call his spirit back into it again."

"Bran has already gone. Meanwhile we will be getting him back to Dun."

And one of the herd riders came forward and crouched at the Queen's feet. "Lady, it was none of our doing, the thunder frightened the herd."

Boudicca looked down at him dully. "Do you think you would still be alive to tell me so, if I had thought for one instant that the fault was yours? Back on your horse, now, and away after the rest. You will be till sundown rounding them up as it is." Her eyes had gone back to Prasutagus's face before she finished speaking. And she knelt down and wiped the blood from it with her own rain-wet hair.

So the companions made a carrying litter of cloaks tied over their spear shafts, and carried the Lord Prasutagus back under the hissing rain. There was no more thunder; it was as though the storm had served the purpose for which it came. And we followed, leading our horses. And all the way, Boudicca walked beside the litter. "Pile more cloaks on him," she said once, "his body will grow too cold for his spirit to come back into it." And that was the only word she spoke, all the way back to the Dun.

They carried him into the Royal Chamber, and laid him down on the bedplace, and the Healer Priests came and felt him over with probing fingers, and with ears laid to his breast, after the manner of their kind. They burned strange things in a pot set so that the smoke fronded across his face and when he breathed he must draw it into himself, and they spread green wound-salve on linen and bound it over his many hurts. And most of that night the chief of the Healers sat beside him, pointing the Fingers of Power sometimes at his head, sometimes at his heart, to strengthen his body so that it could wait for him and receive him back again; for the hoof blow on the side of his head had driven him very far away.

And all the night long, Boudicca squatted at his other side and neither moved nor spoke, nor took her eyes from his face.

Towards dawn he began to stir uneasily, and crouching in the doorway, I heard the Healer Priest let go a long breath like one that is very tired. "He is coming back."

And then Prasutagus turned his head on the fine blue woollen pillows, and threw up all that was in him, as I have known to happen with other men after a blow on the head. And then he called out, fumblingly, "Boudicca! Boudicca!" in a voice that I had never heard from him before; a seeking and longing and desperate voice, as though he were crying out after her through a dark forest.

And she said quickly, "I am here, Love. Feel now; hold to my hands – I am here." And she too spoke in a voice that I had never heard before.

For many days and nights, Prasutagus lay sick and fevered, even while his hurts began to heal, tended night and day by Boudicca herself and her old nurse, and with the Healer Priests coming and going about the Royal Chamber. And then one morning I heard him laugh; a small cracked laugh, for his flanks and breast-cage were still too bruised and battered for him to draw breath easily; but joyous. And I knew that all would be well.

More days went by, and then one night, passing the

entrance to the Royal Chamber with its embroidered deerskin curtain drawn close, on my way to the warm corner of the Hall that was my own sleeping place, I chanced to look down; and there, in the last light of the torches and the white shaft of autumn moonlight falling from the nearest of the high window-holes, the old King's sword with the hilt of nawhal ivory lay across the threshold.

5

To Be a King and Think Too Much

Boudicca no longer carried her head as though her neck were for ever braced to the weight and balance of the moon headdress. Now she walked like one wearing a midsummer garland. There was a bloom on her in the years that followed, and she gave off warmth and happiness as a flower gives off scent. I think that I have never known any woman happy as she was happy in those years. After the babes came, she even grew a little fat. She knew it, and laughed and said, "Where is the use of having little cubs, and no soft lap to nurse them in?"

Essylt the Royal Daughter was born in the dark of winter, pink and squalling, with feathery hair on her head as red as the midwinter fires; and three summers later came Nessan, the little dark one who scarcely ever cried. And each time there was a small fret and tumult in the women's quarters, because Old Nurse would have each babe in turn all to herself as she had had Boudicca; and the Queen, though she would share them, made it very clear that they were hers. Many's the time I have seen her sitting in the sunshine on the threshold of the women's quarters, with her tunic slipped down from her breast, feeding first her fiery baby and then later the little dark one, while Essylt, grown to toddling size, played with a hound puppy at her feet; and her lovely happiness like a cloak about them all. And then maybe Prasutagus's shadow would fall across them as he passed by, and he would check, he looking down and she looking up, and something would pass between them, a kind of shimmer in the air. Once, laughing, he told her, "You look as contented as a cat with her kittens, half-asleep there in the sunshine." And she narrowed her eyes and stroked her cheek against the little dark head of Nessan who she was holding over her shoulder, and said, "Prrr?" softly in her throat.

Aye, those were good years.

And as good years and bad alike must do, they went by.

Rome's yoke sat light enough about our necks. So light at first we scarcely knew it for a yoke at all. Once a year the tax-gatherers came for their tribute of gold and horses. Once a year the agreed number of young braves went off to serve as auxiliaries with the Eagles. But there were always plenty who were glad enough to go, for the adventure and the soldier's pay and the seeing of distant places. Up and down the tribal lands north and west of us, the Red Crests had built their forts. Great far-off forts for the frontier legions, and small ones scattered between, to hold the conquered tribes quiet, like the studs on a shield that hold the dappled oxhide to the wooden backing. But there were no forts in the runs of the Horse People. We were a free people still.

Life took on a more Roman colour; and as the merchants came and went, there began to be more Roman things to be seen. A paved floor with a coloured pattern on it, wine jugs of red Samian ware on a chieftain's table, and maybe a graceful bronze lamp in his women's quarters; though nothing so beautiful as the Queen's dark Bride Cup with the flame at its heart. But we were a free people still.

And then, some six years after we made our friendship treaty with the Emperor at Camulodunum, the first trouble came.

In that winter, Ostorius Scapula, who was Governor of Britain – for the Romans behave as though we were one land and one people divided into a few clans; they do not understand that we are the Tribes, and Britain little more than an idea of their own – Ostorius Scapula began the making of a frontier line; road and fosse and string of forts, running all the way from the hunting runs of the Dumnoni in the far south-west, up to their great new fortress they call Lindum beyond the settlements of the Parisi. This was for a defence against the hill tribes beyond, the Bearers of the Blue Warshields, and the Silures who were still carrying on their own war with Caratacus to lead them at that time.

And when the new frontier line was finished, Ostorius Scapula ordered that the tribes lying next behind it on the Roman side should be stripped of their weapons; amongst them ourselves the Iceni, the Lords of the Horse.

The order came, brought by pot-bellied officials guarded by Red Crests lest we tear them into little pieces and feed them to our hunting dogs. At such and such places, on such and such days, the weapons were to be brought in and stacked for Rome to carry away; and any man caught carrying sword or war spear thereafter was to pay for it with death or slavery. "You have no need of weapons," said those pot-bellied officials. "Rome is here to keep order. Rome is here to protect you." And one, standing beside the fire in the Royal Dun itself, said, "Was it not for that you yielded to your Emperor without a blow, six years since?"

We heard them, we who counted ourselves a free people, and our bellies rose within us.

"We are free allies of Rome! We have paid our allotted tribute, we have sent our young men to serve with the Eagles; but by the word of the Emperor himself, we are a free state, not a conquered people like the Catuvellauni, to be ordered to lay down our arms."

Thus said Prasutagus the King, standing also by the fire in his High Hall. He spoke very softly, and his face had gone as white as buttermilk. He always grew pale and deathly quiet when he was angry. But the officials were not knowing that.

"Then you had best send to Rome, and take the matter up with the Emperor himself," said the pot-bellied one. "Meanwhile, these are the orders of Ostorius Scapula, Governor of Britain."

And all men knew that by then Caesar was old and sick and surrounded by evil advisers.

"I must have time to call the Council, that we may speak together upon this matter," Prasutagus said, as quietly as before.

"You have time enough for that. It is half a month before the date set. Only see that when the day comes, the weapons of the Iceni come with it to the appointed places."

But scarcely were the officials gone jingling off with their escort of Red Crests, and before ever the Council could be called, word came that the clans of our south-western runs had risen against the order, and made their strong place among the great fortified banks of the High Chalk that had been raised long since against the Catuvellauni.

It was evening when the word came, brought by a tired man on a tired horse. The evening meal was over – a gloomy meal it had been – and men and women had moved in from their own sides of the Hall to meet and mingle according to our custom when the eating is done; but there was little of the usual talk and laughter. I sat in my accustomed place at the Queen's feet, my harp tuned and ready, though it was in my mind that there would be no harp music that night. But though it had been quiet before, I mind the deeper quiet that came over the Hall when the news was spoken. And the Queen cried out into it, "Fools! The fools! Could they not have waited at least for word from the Royal Dun?"

Prasutagus set down the cup that he was holding, and got to his feet beside her; and standing there by the fire, he called to his armour-bearer to make ready his war-gear; gave orders for horses to be bridled and chariot teams harnessed up; and sent riders to gather the men of the Kindred, the Royal Clan.

"Let you wait till morning," one of the old men said. "Dawn comes early at this time of year."

"Not early enough! Maybe we are already too late; but assuredly there is no time to wait for morning."

Boudicca also had risen to her feet, and stood facing him. "What will you do?"

"I do not know," he said. "Whatever seems best; whatever there is that can be done."

"I will come and help you to arm," she said.

"No need. Cadog is my armour-bearer."

"But I am your woman," said Boudicca.

And they went together into the Royal Chamber.

Then there was a great coming and going; a flaring of torches all across the outer court, and a trampling of chariot teams being led under the yoke, and the whitt-whitt-whitt of sword and spear blade on the tall black weapon-stone. Cold and blue-white are the sparks that fly from a whetted sword blade; frost-coloured against the red flare of the torches. And the south gates were opened wide, and in the dark hour of the young-summer night, Prasutagus and his household warriors were gone, drumming out over the causeway to meet the war-bands he had summoned to join him along the way.

And behind them was the silence again, and the waiting.

Nine days, we waited, and on the evening of the ninth day they came back, clattering in between the stone gateposts under a low squally sunset barred with yellow along the west; and the yellow made a cold and hollow glitter on their weapons and horse-ornaments. We saw no riderless horses, no empty chariots, and yet they had about them no look of victory. And I was minded of the time we came back from Camulodunum, Prasutagus having done the bitter work of the Council. But then, he had been little more than a boy. He was a man now, and whatever had been done, the doing had been his and not the Council's.

He reined in and got down from his chariot, stiffly, before the threshold where Boudicca waited for him. He was mired with long hard driving, his eyes red-rimmed.

She asked no question, but he answered her as though she had. "The Red Crests stormed the defences. It was all over before we got there."

"What did you do, my Lord?"

"I did what I could. There is some kind of patched-up peace. Pray to our Lady of the Foals that it lasts. At least we are still a free state."

"And the Governor's orders?"

"The Governor's order still stands." The great weariness that was on him sounded in his voice.

The first of the appointed days came for the handing in of weapons; and each clan brought its war-gear in to the steading of its chieftain, where the officials and their Red Crests waited. And in the forecourt of the Royal Dun, Prasutagus brought his own sword, and broke it across his knee; and laid the pieces with deep and formal courtesy at the feet of the senior official. And behind him, one after another, the warriors of the Royal Clan did the like; until the pile rose so high and wide that the official must step back quickly to avoid losing a toe or two, and someone in the gathering laughed.

So it was done, swords broken, spearheads wrenched from their shafts and flung into the waiting carts. By evening, all was over.

I wondered if they must be fed and lodged in the Royal Dun for the night, as we had fed and lodged the tribute-collectors every year. But the Red Crests, following their usual custom, had made their own camp for the night; and I am thinking the officials felt safer within their stockade than within ours. And I am thinking that maybe for that time they were right.

Next day, after they were gone, and their laden carts with them, I took my harp and went away down into the marsh country, for my heart was sore within me, and I needed the space and emptiness, that I might make a lament to ease the ache, with none but the shore birds to hear me.

So towards evening I sat on the bank of a looping waterway, staring down into the water that riffled through the tufted reeds, with my harp fallen silent on my knee. And as I sat there, there was a brushing and flurrying through the reeds, and Prasutagus's two great hounds came along the bank, and lay down with lolling tongues beside me. "Greetings brother, greetings sister," I said. And Prasutagus came up behind them. At most times he was like the rest of his kind, a man who never walked when he could ride or drive. But there were times of darkness, he had, maybe times when the kingship irked him, when he would whistle up the dogs, and take a light hunting spear in his hand – for the look of the thing, even to himself, I think, for he never brought back any kill at such times – and walk until he had outdistanced the darkness in himself. He looked now as if he had walked from the world's end to the world's end, and floundered into a few soft patches on the way. Even the dogs were weary. Maybe, I thought, it was the same with him as with me, only that he had no harp-skill.

He thrust one of the hounds out of the way and sat down beside me, his arms across his knees. "No greeting for me?" he said.

"Greetings, brother," I said. A harper speaks to all living things as equals.

He reached out and touched the nearest horn of my harp with the extreme tip of one forefinger. "A new song for tonight?"

I shook my head. "I make only for myself today – a lament for broken swords."

We were silent a moment, only the pale feathery tips

of the reeds swayed against the drifting sky; and somewhere an oyster-catcher made his lonely whistling call. Then Prasutagus gave a little dry cough. Quite a small sound, but when I looked round, his eyes were shut, and it seemed to me that there was a faint greyness round his mouth.

"Is there something amiss?" I asked, quickly.

He opened his eyes and smiled. Already the greyness was passing. "Nothing. A pain under my ribs and a moment's darkness. It comes on me sometimes after a day's hunting or the like." He turned back to the thing we had been speaking of. "A lament for broken swords. And yet it seems that yourself, you had no sword to lose, yesterday. Strange, I could have sworn that I have seen you burnishing an old sword before now."

"I carried a sword when Boudicca's mother and the world and I were all young. Few people remember now. Few harpers are fighting men, and the Romans would expect no sword from me."

"And so you did not bring them one." He turned and looked at me; a long, hard look.

"Like the Queen, who they would expect no sword from, either," I said, and wondered in that moment, where she had hidden her father's great blade. Under the gowns in her clothes' kist, maybe. No, she would have been more thorough than that.

"I wonder how many old swords are hidden in the peat-stacks and under the house-thatch of the Iceni today," Prasutagus said.

"More than the Romans dream. Spearheads, too – though indeed there is none so great a difference between a war-spear and a heavy hunting-spear, when once the collar of heron hackles has been stripped away. They did not even notice that none of the women came in, for they do not train their own women to bear weapons in time of need."

"That is true. Maybe we are not so toothless as they think us." But almost as he said it, he struck his fist on his knee. "Grief upon me! I speak comforting words to myself as though I were a bairn! The Horse People, I make no doubt, have good store of weapons yet, hidden in the dark. But in the daylight, before the eyes of Rome, before the eyes of other tribes, we are disarmed and dishonoured! And that is my doing."

"The order was from Ostorius Scapula," I said.

And again we were silent, hearing the wind in the feathered reeds. And Fand, the brindled bitch, daughter to one of the hounds who had come with him from his own hunting runs eight years ago, raised her head and whimpered softly, looking at her Lord.

"The order was from Scapula, yes," Prasutagus agreed at last. "But it was with me to choose whether or no it should be obeyed. There was a moment – I could have set fire to the stubble. I could have had the whole Horse People out in revolt, and maybe driven the Red Crests back into the soft lands to the south."

"What happened?"

"I started to think."

"What kind of thinking?"

"That the Red Crests do not take easily to defeat, no more easily than the Tribes; and that they can always send for help from across the seas, for they are as many as the leaves of the forest, that though they fall in the autumn come again in the spring. I began to think of burned thatch and hearths left desolate with no man to come home to them."

"It is you that should be the harper, not I."

"I wish I were," Prasutagus said. And again he turned full face to me. "It is not easy to be a king and think too much. In another kind of world, maybe. . . .But in our world, a king should leave his thinking to his Harper and the Priest Kind. It would be easier to bear. He might even be a better king, that way."

"Despite the burned thatch and the hearths left desolate?"

"We should have gone down with honour, by the Warrior's Road," he said. And then, "I do not know. Cadwan of the Harp, there are so many things that I do not know."

6
Day Draws to Sunset

The winters came, and the springs woke in the alders, and the mares dropped their foals in early summer, all as it had been before the Horse People were stripped of the right to carry sword and spear. And year by year we paid our tribute of gold and horses and young men.

No more children were borne in the Royal Chamber; but the two Princesses grew and flourished. Essylt, the Royal Daughter, fair-skinned and freckled like a foxglove, blue-eyed and long-boned like her mother; like her mother in most other ways too, both within and without; only from Prasutagus her father she had her hair that was the colour of a bay horse in the sunlight. And Nessan, the little one, born while the midsummer fires were blazing. And Nessan was nobody but herself – unless she had in her some Princess of the Old People, the Little Dark People, who were here before ever the Horse Folk came; for there was never yet a conquering people that did not mingle their blood in some sort with the blood of the conquered. Old Nurse swore that it was so; but Old Nurse was of the Dark People herself. Nessan was bird-small, with black hair and huge rain-grey eyes, and her milk teeth came crooked, so that the teeth that came after them were crooked too, though it only showed when she laughed. I loved to see her laugh, the little dark one, just as I loved to hear her sing. She could sing like a bird in a white-thorn tree, less full than a blackbird, softer than a robin, a thrush maybe.

When ever she could escape from the Women's Side, Essylt would be away to the stable court, or watching the smith hammering out a hunting-spear, or down in the marsh making a fish trap with Duatha, whose father was chief of the household warriors, when she could persuade him to let her come. But Nessan would come to me and my harp; for she had the music in her. "Since you are not the Royal Daughter," I told her, "you should have been a boy, and then you could have been harper to a Queen."

In the world beyond our frontiers, Caratacus, after nine years' warfare in the western hills, had gone to walk in chains in a Roman triumph, betrayed into the Red Crests' hands by the Queen of the Brigantes; but that is another story altogether.

Ostorius Scapula was gone, too, and we had a new Governor, Suetonius Paulinus; a great soldier, so said his reputation, following him from the ends of the Empire; but a hard man like an east wind and a hammer.

And in Rome, the old Emperor was dead; some said by poison at the hands of his wife; and a new Emperor reigned in his stead: a man with music in him, even as I, but possessed by spirits of darkness. It is far, from Rome to the frontiers of the Horse People, but we began to feel his darkness hovering over us. We felt it through new laws and regulations that ate away our remaining freedom, through the officials and the money-lenders. The harvests had been poor for three years running, and many of the great chiefs were in debt – yet it was more than these things, and it lay over more tribes than the Horse People. An unease, a sense of dread like the silence that comes over the furze beneath the shadow of a wheeling hawk.

But still, the ordinary things of life went on. And the time came, when Essylt had seen fifteen summers, and Nessan two summers less, to be holding the Choosing Feast for the Royal Daughter. So the feast was held, and Merddyn Oak Priest, who began to be too old for such duties, slept his night on a freshly-flayed horsehide in the apple garth; and the choice fell upon Duatha, he that was son to Arviragus, chief of the King's companions. A tall, hot-blooded lad he was, with his manhood scars still fresh upon him. And for Essylt and Duatha the choice was a happy one, for they had been close to each other since the fish-trap days, though I have sometimes thought more in the way of brother and sister than in the way of two who will one day be man and woman to each other.

Grief upon me! It all seems so long past, and it is just the one year ago.

One day, not long after the Choosing Feast, Roman officials came to the Dun when it was not time for the collecting of taxes, on some private business with Prasutagus. And in the evening of the next day, when they had gone again, I walked in the in-paddock, which has always been dear to me on early autumn evenings, when the brood mares are gathered close with their foals, and the dusk lies like smoke under the alder trees, and the smell of the first frost is in the air. And Prasutagus came by, driving a new chariot that he had been trying out. He reined in and got down when he saw me, and we began to walk back towards the Dun, leaving the charioteer to take on the team.

"So – that is over," said Prasutagus.

"The Romans?"

"The Romans."

"What did they come for?"

"I have been making my will. That is what they call it, among the Romans, when a man has it written down before witnesses, what is to be done with his goods and gear, after he has gone beyond the sunset."

"Was that needful?" I asked.

"I think so, yes. Since my father died, I am a rich man, my horse-herds as big as those of the Queen herself, maybe bigger, if the mares do well this year. And I have done what a great many rich men do in these days; I have left half of what I possess to the Emperor – in the hope of buying his favour, so that my wife and the young ones may keep the other half in peace."

"You have not a grey hair as yet, in that red poll of yours," I said quickly.

And he laughed, "And there may be a score more Emperors come and gone in Rome before my time comes for the Long Journey." Then he grew sober. "But these are uncertain days, and the Emperor Nero is not the Emperor Claudius. It is better to make plans for the night while the daylight lasts."

The smoke of the evening cooking-fires was hanging low over the roofs of the village and the Dun as we came to the small side-gate into the chariot court.

Prasutagus swung away to see his team stabled, walking proud with life, then he checked an instant and put out a hand to the corner-post of the long chariot shed, and I heard again that small dry cough. Then he walked on into the gathering dusk.

On a day towards winter's end, Prasutagus and his hearth companions called for their horses and whistled up their hounds and went hunting.

It was a day that started fair, but turned to wind and sleety rain; and they returned at evening with a couple of red forest deer slung across the backs of the carrying ponies, but themselves drenched and wild and sodden as though they had been hunting with Blue Haired Mananon along the seabed.

They dismounted in the chariot court, and Prasutagus looked round for Fand, who was daughter to that other, old Fand, and his favourite bitch as her mother had been before her. She had not gone out with the hunt, being heavy in whelp and near her time. But always she would come running to him when he had been away, to bury her muzzle between his hands, whimpering with delight at his return. But this evening she did not come, and he called for her, and then for the chief of the kennel slaves. "Baruch! Where is Fand?"

The man came out of the shadows. "Back there behind the fodder store, and the pups are coming."

"In this weather? Man, have you not the sense to get her into shelter?"

"She'll not come – and I am afraid to rough-handle her – "

"Is something amiss?" Prasutagus demanded.

The old slave shook his head. "She was well enough with the first two. She is in trouble with this one."

"I'll come," Prasutagus said.

When he did not come into Hall with the rest, and Duatha told the Queen what had happened, she looked at the drenched companions steaming by the fire, and sent out his armour-bearer to bid him come into the warmth and get him dry and some hot food inside him. "It will not take long, and then he can be going back to Fand," she said, as though she were his mother.

But the armour-bearer returned alone. "My Lord Prasutagus says that he will come in a while and a while," he said.

But it was a long while; and when he came, and the evening meal half over, he was like the ghost of one long drowned in wintry seas; grey white to the lips, his clothes hanging on him as coldly sodden as sea-wrack. He came to the fire, holding out his hands to the flames; and they had blood on them, and they shook.

Boudicca went to him. "Hai Mai! You are the wet one! Let you come now and change those sodden rags."

"In a little," he said.

And Essylt, close behind her mother, asked him, "Father, how is it with Fand?"

"She's dead. It will be well enough with the cubs, if Baruch can find them a foster mother." And he turned from the fire towards the entrance to the Royal Chamber, where his armour-bearer waited for him.

When he came back, in fresh tunic and breeks, his hair standing out in spikes where he had rubbed it dry, he went again to the fire; and Boudicca herself brought him food and wine from the table, that he might eat beside the blaze. But he ate only a few mouthfuls of the food, then pushed it aside and drank the wine. It seemed that he could not stop shivering.

"This is a cheerless fire that we have tonight," he said, and forced a grin. "It looks bright enough, but somebody must have cast a spell on it, for it gives out no heat."

I felt a faint movement against my knee, and when I looked down, Nessan, who was sitting there as she ften did in the evenings, was looking up at me, with rouble in those strange rain-grey eyes of hers."Is he ick?" she asked at half breath.

"He is chilled to the bone, and he has just lost his avourite hound. If Epona grant it, a night's rest will ee him well again, little bird."

But next morning did not see Prasutagus well again. Ie was flushed as he had been grey the night before, nd with a small wracking cough that grew worse as he day went by. And by evening it could be seen that ie found it hard to catch his breath.

"It is the lung fever," said the Healer Priest, and hook his head.

"He is very strong!" Boudicca said. "Stronger than he lung fever."

And again the Priest shook his head, "There is an cho in his heart that should not be there. I first heard t when I listened to the life within his chest, seventeen utumns ago."

"If it has been with him so long, it can make no lifference now," said the Queen, with terror in her oice.

And a third time the Healer Priest shook his head. 'We will do all that can be done. We will make the Sacrifices. But it is an old friend. Truly every man valks with death from the moment that he is born."

And Prasutagus lay on the great bedplace, propped igh with the coloured pillows, trying to laugh without enough breath to laugh with, and telling the riests that it was only a pain in his chest that would ass by and by, and they were no more than a gaggle of old women.

And all the while, for three days and three nights, he wind blew, howling round the High Hall, and the freezing rain drenched down. But on the third night the rain ceased and the wind died away, and the silence was filled with the faint trickling of waters; and in the air outside was the faint unmistakable smell which is the promise of spring as yet far off. And in the dark heart of that night, Prasutagus died.

Boudicca and Old Nurse had tended him throughout, as they had done that first time, seventeen years before. And at first, Boudicca would not believe that what had happened that first time would not happen this time also. "Pile more rugs on him!" she said. "We must keep him warm for his spirit to come back to!"

And Old Nurse, weeping and clinging to her, said, "Hush, hush now, come away. This time his spirit will not come back."

But Boudicca lay rigid along the bedplace, holding him in her arms, not seeming to feel the old woman pulling at her, calling and calling for more rugs to keep him warm.

Essylt had stolen away somewhere, to Duatha, I am thinking, for what ever comfort he could be giving her. Aiee! The pair of children! But Nessan had come to me, just beyond the threshold, and I held her close while she shivered in my arms. "I wish she would not – Oh I wish she would not! Cannot someone stop her?"

"Maybe you could stop her," I said. "Let you go and try."

And she went in, the little one, into the chamber where the Priests had begun the journey rituals, and the King lay dead; and I do not think that she spoke at all. But her arms did what Old Nurse's could not do; and in a while the Queen got up and allowed them to lead her away.

To the Lady Julia Procilla, at the House of the Three Walnut Trees. In Massilia, Province of Southern Gaul. From Gneus Julius Agricola, in Britain, Greeting.

Most dear Mother, When I came away, you bade me promise to write as often as might be. See now what a dutiful son I am! You also bade Marcipor to look after me as a good body-slave should do; but in truth, I seem to have done little but look after him, for he developed saddle boils on the way up through Gaul, and was direly seasick during the crossing. Anyhow, here we are, safe and sound, having landed at Rhutupiae, and come on to Londinium riding post. Tomorrow I shall buy a couple of horses and baggage beasts – they tell me the horse market here is good – and then join the next mounted party heading for Deva, where I learn the Governor now is.

Meanwhile, I am lodged in the house of Decianus Catus, the Procurator, which is better than the Government resthouse. Catus is in fact the soul of hospitality; but only, I should judge, to those he thinks may be in a position to repay him in one way or another in the future. He is, after all, a business man, even though a business man in Government service. Dearest Mother, you are perfectly right, it is ungentlemanly to be rude about one's host. But you brought me up to be truthful, and the truth is that I do not like the man, and I do not think Father would have liked him either. It is strange, considering that Father was killed in the summer that I was born, how well I seem to know him. That must be because you brought me up knowing him; and since I never thought to thank you for that before, I will thank you now. He was clearly so well worth knowing. But to return to Decianus Catus; it is really very good of him to give me guestroom, for he is especially busy at the moment: one of the native rulers, Prasutagus, King of a free state somewhere north of here, is dead this past month or more, and the Emperor has given orders for the state to be abolished, and the tribe and its territory absorbed into the ordinary pattern of provincial government. He is doing that all over the Empire, of course; and I suppose that since this Prasutagus has no son to follow him, and the royal line is at an end, this is the obvious time for it to happen to the Iceni also. So says Decianus Catus, at all events. It seems hard; but no one thinks there will be trouble. For one thing, the Iceni are unarmed – after trouble some years ago – and have no one to lead them. But apparently the money-lenders who have been busy among them are calling in the debts to be on the safe side; Seneca foremost among them. How odd that a philosopher preaching the virtues of the simple life should turn to that particular trade.

Forgive me. I started this letter by criticizing my host, and now I am criticizing a friend of Father's, and one to whose good offices, at least in part, I owe my place as a tribune on the Governor's Staff – you must blame it on the weather. Here we are into the first days of March; and at home the almond trees will be in flower and the vines sprouting. But here there is no sign of spring at all; at least, none that my southern-bred eyes can make out. Admittedly, we were blind with wind and rain all the way from Rhutupiae, and so I have seen little but this town. It's something of a shanty town still, lacking in roots. Well of course none of it is more than eighteen years old, even the army depot, and you can't expect many roots in that time. But it seems prosperous enough; lots of shipping below the bridge; so there should be a few reasonable wine shops around.

And even as I write, a wing of blue sky has appeared behind the roof of the shiny new temple everybody is so proud of. I think I shall go out and explore. . . .

7
The Queen's Awakening

So the death-fires blazed for King Prasutagus, and his ashes were laid in the Royal House of Sleep, his shield – the Romans had left us our shields – and his best wolf spear made fine with a war collar of fierce blue-black heron's feathers, for his journey. But no sword. Even for the King, the Horse People could not spare a sword. And the moon that had been new when he died, waxed full and waned into the dark, and was new again.

And all that time, Boudicca was like one bound by a spell. Some spell of the old Earthling magic such as the Dark People know how to cast. She did all that was needed of a Priest-Queen, as surely as she had always done it. She walked from place to place about the Dun, braced and erect as though always, now, she carried the weight of the moon headdress upon her head. She sat listening in her place at the Council Fire, and answered any who spoke to her. She even ate a little, sitting in her High Place at the evening meal. But when you looked at her, nothing looked back out of her eyes, and the glow of warmth and life that had always come from her came no more. It was Old Nurse and the other women who did what they could to comfort the young ones, and maybe Duatha and myself, a little, too, in our different ways. And maybe in some sort they comforted each other. It was as though Boudicca their mother was not there at all; as though, having left her outer shape to move and speak for her in the world of the living, she herself had gone to lie in the Place of Sleep with Prasutagus, along with his shield and spear. And there were times, as the new moon began to wax once more, when I wondered, and I think not I alone, whether she would ever wake again.

And then at the full moon of Corn Sowing, the Romans came.

We were well used to the visits of the tax-collectors and their kind; but this was another thing. This was Decianus Catus the Procurator himself. He who had been only a name and a grasping shadow to us until that day; and with him more Government officials than ever we had seen in the same place at the same time before, and an escort of Red Crests more than two hundred strong.

Word of their coming had raced ahead of them to reach us in the usual way. But it was the time of the full moon offering; the little offering of grain and mares' milk which every woman makes for her household, and the Queen for all her tribe. And so at the moment of their coming, she was elsewhere, and they must wait in the Hall, the Red Crests drawn up and leaning on their spears in the forecourt. And they did not like to wait. You could see them chafing under their Roman calm.

She came soon enough, the Princesses behind her, and the Moon Mark still chalk-drawn on her forehead. To us, it is a thing of great beauty, the Moon Mark, three-winged like an iris flower, springing from between the brows. But they looked at it as though it were the ploy of some foolish child. And the Procurator began without greeting, "Did your people not tell you who was in your hall? I am a busy man, and do not like to be kept waiting."

"They told me," Boudicca said, "but the Lady, also, does not like to be kept waiting."

And she took the Guest Cup from Essylt, and held it out to him.

"Drink and be welcome."

And when he had drunk, she sat herself in the High Place; I in my usual place at her feet – that is the fine thing, being a harper, that when your harp is silent you can be as little noticed as a hound under the table – and rug-covered stools and more wine were brought for the Procurator and his officers.

A man stood by to turn Roman and British speech to and fro between the speakers, but there was little need of him, for the Procurator spoke the tongue of the Tribes after a fashion, and with the passing of the years, we have come to know something of the Latin tongue also.

Then Decianus Catus took a scroll from the young man who stood beside him, and gave it to the Queen.

She took and unrolled it and looked at the written words, then let it spring back, and handed it again to the Procurator. "Your tongue, I can speak a little, but I cannot read it when it is written down. Let you tell me what this writing says."

The Procurator took the scroll, and once more unrolled it. But his eyes never moved along the lines of written words. I could see that he knew by heart what was in the scroll, and that what was in it pleased him well, though he took care to keep a grave official face.

"Lady, this writing says that now your husband Prasutagus is dead, leaving no sons, and the Royal

Line of the Iceni at an end, the Divine Emperor Nero has decided upon doing away with the free state over which he ruled, and absorbing the people and territory of the Iceni into the Province of Britain, under the same form of government as any other part of the Empire. He bids you to accept his will in this matter, and obey the commands of his officers sent to carry it out."

He spoke loudly and clearly, and his words reached the companions gathered at the lower end of the Hall. I saw the sudden movement among them, the quickly raised heads, the in-caught breath. But I thought for a moment that they had not reached Boudicca at all. Then she said, almost dreamily, "I am the Queen. Here beside me are my daughters, the Royal Line of the Iceni is not at an end."

The Procurator smiled. Small white teeth, he had, very even; but there seemed to be too many of them in his mouth. "As to that, Imperial Rome takes no account of Queens, only of Kings."

Boudicca rose slowly to her feet and stood looking down at him with those empty eyes that might have frightened a wiser man. "I am thinking that Imperial Rome may have good cause to take account of *this* Queen!" she said.

"Threats, from those without power, have a hollow sound." The Procurator tapped the scroll with his fingers. "There is more. Would you hear it?"

"I would hear it, that I may know all that comes against the Horse People."

"Ah no, this does not concern the Horse People, only yourself and your daughters."

Behind her, I saw the Princesses move closer together.

"I make no doubt you know already that your late husband in his will named the Divine Emperor as heir to his personal fortune."

"Half his personal fortune," said the Queen.

"Ah, to be sure. But the Emperor makes no doubt that that was an oversight. You and your daughters will have enough, far more than enough, in your own right, even from the sale of your jewels if need be, to live quietly, as you will be living from now on. If it were not so, the Emperor would of course provide you with a small state pension. But he is extremely short of money just at present. The citizens of Rome require a great many circuses to keep them happy, and circuses are not cheap. Divine Caesar is convinced that your late husband did not leave him his whole fortune simply because he was not aware of this." His smile broadened, showing yet more teeth. "And so, rather than take offence at the oversight, he has resolved to take the will for the deed, and accept the whole. I am commanded to attend to all matters concerning the collection of his inheritance."

Boudicca went on looking at him. Then she said in that cool, almost gentle voice, "Your mother must have wept for shame on the day she bore you."

He made a tiny movement as though the farthest tip of a whiplash had flicked him. But still he kept his smooth official manner, and for the moment there was mockery in his tone. "Ah now, I cry your mercy, Lady! Remember I am but the Emperor's Procurator, carrying out the Emperor's orders."

"I do remember that," said Boudicca. "Little man, it is easy to remember." And then, "My Lord's wealth was for the most part in horses and cattle, after the way of our people. Brood mares and half-wild colts and unbroken stallions. Have you brought enough herd riders with you to handle such a legacy?"

"They need not all be run south in one drove; and for the first, a few herding slaves in part payment –"

"Our herds are handled by free men of the people."

He made an impatient gesture. "These are trifling matters, to be dealt with at another time."

"Surely," said the Queen. "But the other thing that is in the Emperor's scroll, the first thing, that is no trifling matter."

And all the while I was thinking, "This is not Boudicca, this creature of dream-bound calm. None of this is Boudicca." And I was cold afraid, and missed what came after, until the Procurator and his men were getting to their feet.

Decianus Catus was saying, "Meanwhile the hour draws on to supper time. Will you give orders for meal and oil and wine to be issued to the Escort, and bid your slaves to show us to our sleeping places, that we may wash off the dust of the road, before we eat?"

"Your Escort shall be fed," said the Queen. "Where is it that you and your fellows think to eat?"

"This, that was your husband's hall, will do well enough."

"As it pleases you. My daughters and I will eat in the women's quarters."

"Ah no, to eat and yet lack the pleasure of female company, that is but half a meal. Where is your British hospitality? Besides, it may be that some of these matters of which we have spoken, trifling or no, may be sorted out more smoothly across the supper table."

"This also is an order?" said the Queen.

"It is."

"Another of the Divine Emperor's?"

"No, of mine, my Lady Boudicca."

She gave him back look for look. "You are not afraid?"

"To eat at your table? With more than two centuries of legionnaries outside? With the power of Imperial Rome behind me, which likes not to have its ministers murdered in stray corners of the Empire and does not leave them lying unavenged? You are no fool, Lady; you will think of burned thatch and salted fields, and men sold into slavery. No, Lady, I am not afraid. I look forward to a pleasant evening in the company of yourself and your most fair daughters."

So Boudicca gave the needful orders; and when the Procurator and his men were gone to the guest-huts, with slaves to tend upon them, she went like one walking in her sleep, to the Royal Chamber; and the two Princesses close behind her. And as they walked, I saw Nessan reach out for her sister's hand, and Essylt take it in a quick hard clasp. I think that was the first time I had seen them go hand in hand since they were bairns. I bided by the fire. She would know where to find me if she had need of me. And sure enough, before long one of the women came running, "Hurry! The Queen bids you come."

And when I came into the Royal Chamber, the Queen stood in the midst of the place, her clenched fists driven against her temples on either side, as though to hold her head from flying apart. Her women and the Princesses stood against the walls, watching her with curd-white faces. "I am in the hollow of his hand," she was saying, "and he knows it. May he die a slow death and watch the flesh rot from off his bones while the breath is still in him!"

Her hair that she had torn down, hung forward about her face, so that I could not see it; but I knew that she was awake from her long sleep.

Old Nurse said, "I have certain skills that you know of. The skills of the Dark People. I can give you a little powder to put into his food, but with so short time, I cannot come by enough for the others."

"No poison," said the Queen. "It may be that I will come to you for your skills, one day, but that will be for myself, not for the Procurator Decianus Catus."

"It would be good, that he should die," said Old Nurse, simply.

"It would be good! But not for the Horse People. At least, not yet."

"What, then, are you thinking?" one of the women asked.

"Of burned thatch and salted fields and men sold into slavery. But I must have time to think of other things." She turned and saw me, and thrust the hair back from her face. "Time to think of many things – to make sure that if the thing comes to fighting, we do not fight in vain. Cadwan, go to the companions; I saw their faces as they stood by the door. Tell them to bring no hidden weapons to supper. Ah, but when did that ever stop trouble, since men must have their knives to eat with. . . .Tell them, then, that this evening must pass in seeming peace. That nothing must happen to fire the stubble, before the Queen has had time for her thinking."

And as I hesitated in the doorway, not sure if there was any other word for me, she turned to her women, "Old Nurse, bring me my gold and cornelian necklace, and the Queen's arm rings; the Princesses' jewels, also. Caer, my red and purple gown – and the box with the eyepaint."

They stared at her, gaping, and she began to laugh, wildly. "He seeks to humiliate us. That is why we are forced to sup with him. He shall see whether he can reach high enough to humiliate the Royal Women of the Iceni!"

And she went to the clothes' kist from which the woman Caer had just shaken out the heavy red and purple gown, and herself lifted from among the folds of other gowns and mantles stored there, a bundle wrapped in the finest crimson cloth. And a little gasp ran through the chamber. Always, on the greatest occasions and for the most honoured guests, the green cup with the fire at its heart was brought out. Essylt cried out, "Mother! No!"

And the Queen turned on her like a wildcat, so that she shrank back, "Little fool! I would smash it to pieces with my own hand, before he lay so much as a finger on it!" Then to Rhun she said, "Old Nurse, set down the jewels. There is no knowing what the outcome of this Roman visit will be; therefore take this and lay it away safe beside my father's sword, until the house is clean of these wolf-spawn!"

And I saw that there was no other word for me, and I went to find the companions.

8

Death on the Dancing Floor

So with the full dark, when they were washed and had put on fresh garments, the Roman officials and the Commander of their Escort came again to sup in the High Hall, and Boudicca came out to them with the Princesses and her women behind her.

And truly it seemed that the fire on the hearths leapt up to greet her, and she walking tall and proud in her red and purple gown with the Queen's goldwork about her arms and neck, and her eyes stained with the green malachite eyepaint that she scarcely ever wore, and all the bones of her face (she was lean enough, now) standing out hard and beautiful. And behind her, Essylt walked defiant under her blaze of red hair; and Nèssan, the little dark one – nobody but I would have seen that she was afraid, only that her lips were set like a boy's when he comes to his man-making.

The Procurator and his officials had been given their places with the companions on the Men's Side of the Hall, and the Queen greeted them and would have gone to the Queen's Place that had been made ready for her on the Women's Side. But Decianus Catus came from the men's table, holding out his hand. "And must we shout to each other across the fires, with all the width of the hall between us? Ah no, that is no way for a pleasant evening."

"It is the custom of the Tribes, that men and women do not eat together," Boudicca said.

"But this evening, let us follow the custom of Rome. So we may talk together of many things, and enjoy each other's company." He seemed to have laid aside the man who had spoken of burned thatch and salted fields, earlier in the evening. But it was only the outer seeming that had changed. The man was still there. And Boudicca cried out to the slaves to bring forward trestle-boards and stools and benches, and set them up on the Dancing Floor between the two fires.

And when it had been done, they sat down, the Queen and the Princesses, the Roman officials and the Escort Commander all together, while the warriors and the women took their usual places along the sides of the Hall, and the cook-slaves brought the great bronze pots of beef-stew and barley cakes and the tall jars of Greek wine.

"We would have had a boar for you, and badger baked in honey, if we had known that we had guests this night," the Queen said. "This is plain fare, but at least the wine is worthy of Imperial Rome." And she gestured to young Cerdic, who had been Prasutagus's cupbearer, to bring the great bronze cup with the silver rim, and put her lips to it, in courtesy, or in token that it was not poisoned, I am not sure which, and bade him take it to the Procurator.

So the meal went on. And all up and down the sides of the Hall, we watched those who sat at the makeshift cross-table between the fires, with the light of the torches all about them. And Oh, but the Queen was beautiful in the torchlight, like some queen out of the oldest and deepest legends of our people. And I saw that I was not the only one to be thinking so, for the eyes of the Procurator were often upon her, across the rim of the great bronze wine-cup; and it was not all in mockery, when he said, "When all this regrettable business is over, you must be done with this barbarian way of life, and come to us at Camulodunum."

I could hear him well enough, for there was little talk along the side tables, and I saw the fire under her green eyelids. But she only said, "I thought your living place was in Londinium."

"Only for business purposes," he said, "Londinium is a rough place; the business centre of the Province; yet but in truth it is little more than a big sprawling trading post. In Camulodunum there begins to be something of civilization. The great temple to the Divine Claudius, the circus and the theatre – and so many Romans have settled there that it has become almost a little corner of Rome itself, and life has taken on a reasonable degree of comfort. A small house in one of the more pleasant suburbs – you would not be the first British lady to find pleasure in our Roman way of life. And I assure you," he leaned towards her, "you would have no difficulty in finding husbands for your daughters."

And there was truth in that, I thought, seeing how the hot and hungry eyes of the Escort Commander had been on the Princess Essylt all evening; but I doubted if it was of marriage that he was thinking.

Young Duatha was beside me on the bench; and I felt him move sharply, and glanced round; but both his hands were on the table, and his knife was not in them.

Boudicca only said, "Then maybe I will come to Camulodunum – one day. Meanwhile, I am the Royal Woman of the Iceni. And my hearth and my pillar-stone are here among my own people."

Before he could answer her, there came a distant splurge of sound from somewhere in the night outside; voices and ugly laughter, and a woman's protesting cry. The hounds under the tables sprang up, bristling, and men were on their feet, looking towards the doorway. But the foreporch was full of Red Crests. And into the moment's pause, clear through the tangled worry of sound, came the lowing of frightened cattle.

The Queen looked from the Procurator to the crowded doorway and back again. "What evil thing is going forward, out there?"

He remained sprawling in his seat, playing with his wine-cup, and looking round at her with that smile that showed too many teeth. "I should imagine the Escort have found the barley beer you gave them for supper somewhat stronger than the watered wine they are used to. Either that, or they have found their way to the main supply. Nothing that need trouble you unduly."

"Nothing? A woman cried out – and they are driving cattle – "

The Women's Side had risen a while since, the Princesses with them, to carry round the tall-necked wine-jars, in the way of the Tribes when the men have finished eating, and at that same moment Essylt was pouring for the Escort Commander. She checked, her head turned like all others, towards the door. The man's hot, hungry eyes were on her still, and he put out his hand, the arm heavy with military bracelets, to touch her wrist. "Do not be afraid, my flame-flower, no harm shall touch a hair of your bright head while I am by." And his hand began to move further up her arm.

She tried to pull away, but instantly the straying caress turned into a grip that she could not break. She twisted and strained for an instant, then stood still and rigid in his grasp. "Let me go!"

The Queen rose to her feet. In that breath of time, she looked taller than any man there. "Let her go, Commander."

He began to laugh, pulling the Princess closer. "Lady, you should not breed such pretty daughters if you do not want them to be admired!"

Essylt made to dash the wine-jar in his face, but he caught her other wrist, laughing still, and dragged her half across his knee. "Pretty Princess! Pretty vixen! – "

The wine-jar crashed to the Dancing Floor and rolled across it, spilling its crimson stain as it went.

The Queen cried out something, high and furious. I never heard what; all things seemed happening at the same time, and the Escort Commander was laughing still as Duatha beside me took the table at a flying leap, and I saw the torchlight strike fire from the blade of his knife that seemed to have leapt from his belt into his hand. The Red Crest Commander, his laughter left unfinished, sprawled backward off his seat, with blood bubbling from a hole like a second mouth that had opened in his throat, while the Royal Daughter, blood and wine mingled all down the front of her gown, tore herself free. Men had sprung to seize the Queen between them; and one of the Red Crests in the doorway shouted, "Murder!" to the rest in the night behind him; and there was a rush of men. Our own warriors snatching at the daggers with which they had been hacking off their meat so short a time before, and hurling themselves upon those around the Queen. And I caught my own knife from my belt, and made for Nessan, where she stood pressed back against one of the great roof trees, and got her behind me, just as the Red Crests with their short stabbing swords came charging up the Hall.

I stabbed at the firstcomer, but he took the blade on his shield and jabbed the great bronze boss up into my face. All round me, our warriors with no weapon but their knives, were close-locked in battle against the heavy painted shields and deadly short-swords. I knew the shouting and trampling, the great wave of bronze and red that seemed breaking over us, the yelling faces. But I was three-parts blind with blood; and a great blow took me on the side of the head; I was beaten and battered to my knees, and the last thing I heard was Nessan screaming, before the darkness took me.

There was one jagged hole in the darkness; like a rent in a black cloak; and through it, I saw and heard as a man may do in an evil dream, and have no power to move or even cry out, a woman with her back to me and her arms lashed above her head to one of the roof-trees, and her gown torn to below the waist so that her back was bare, and her bright hair tumbled about her shoulders, all blood-dabbled and fouled; and a man-shaped beast in bronze scales standing behind her and to one side, his feet wide-planted, and in his hands a centurion's vine-staff upraised. And even as I watched, he brought it down again across her back – and again – and again. I saw her shudder to each blow, the quivering muscles of her back and shoulders standing out, convulsed, the bloody weals springing on her white skin. She did not cry out under the blows, but a hoarse terrible raving came from her.

And I knew that it was the Queen. The beast in bronze scales checked for a moment, and looked, grinning, towards someone I could not see. And the Procurator's voice said, "Ten more strokes, I think. Yes, ten more should help to quench her fires."

And dead men were lying round me, and others standing with their arms bound behind them and their wounds running red; and somewhere, a girl was still screaming, the terrible high screaming of a wounded hare, that went on, and on. . . .

I struggled to get to my feet to do something, anything; and the world tilted and slid away from me sideways, and the darkness took me again.

9

The Dark Queen

Gradually, out of the darkness grew a grey fog. I was floating up through the fog; and the further up I floated, the worse grew the pain in my head, and the nearer the threat of some horror waiting for me; so that I struggled to get back to the nothingness of the dark; but my struggle seemed only to drive me further up towards the surface, the grey fog thinning all the while. And I was lying on piled fern in my usual sleeping place in one of the side aisles of the Hall. And there was an armourer's hammer beating in my head. I fumbled up one hand to find what was amiss with it, and felt the folds of rag bound round it, and the dryness of crusted blood; and the memory of last night broke over me in a wave. I let out a cry, but I am thinking that it was not from the pain in my head.

Something moved in the shadows, and Old Rhun came crouching down beside me and pulled my hand away. "Leave be!" she said. "Leave be, or you will start the bleeding again; and there are enough dead in the Queen's Hall this day, without that you must be adding to them."

I could only see through one eye, and when I tried to speak through my torn and swollen lips, my tongue seemed made of wood and would not answer to my will. She saw it, and took up a cup and held it to my mouth. I spat away broken teeth, and swallowed clear water, and forced out some kind of croak meant for a question; for many questions.

"The officials and their Red Crests have gone," she said, in a weeping voice. "They have stripped the Dun and emptied the stables and driven off the herds from the in-pastures. They have hauled away slave and free alike, with ropes round their necks. They have speared the very pups in the kennels." And yet I knew that she was telling me only the lesser things, and that there was more and worse to come.

My tongue was returning to me, and returning also, pressing in on me, the memory of that terrible jagged rent in last night's darkness. I managed to force out a few words, "Boudicca – did they – ?"

"They stripped and flogged the Queen, like one of their own garrison sluts caught thieving."

"And – the Princesses?"

The old woman bowed herself together like one in unbearable pain. She seemed to have aged a hundred years since I last saw her in the Royal Chamber. "They used the Princesses as – as men use women captured in war. Ochone! Ochone! They will never be maidens again till the moon stands still in the sky! I would have given them sleep – a little sleep to spread a darkness between them and the thing the soldiers did to them – Aiee! The children that they are! But their mother would not have it so; she will have them to stand beside her; she is without mercy, on them on herself on any living thing – and there is nothing else that I can do."

I dragged myself to my elbow. "Where are they?"

"Out in the forecourt where the warriors are gathering. Na na, lie still, there is nothing that you can do either."

She began clinging to me, and I shook her off and blundered to my feet. The world dipped and swam round me, but the darkness did not come back. Broken benches and trestle-boards lay across my way, and there was a strong acrid smell in the air. A hanging that I caught at to steady myself came down in my hand, charred all along its top; but at last I lurched out into the main Hall. For a moment I could not think why there seemed to be so much daylight in the Hall, the clear, constantly changing light of a spring day when the wind blows from off the sea. And then I saw that the foremost end of the roof was gone, hanging in ragged bat-wings of charred thatch and blackened timbers; and the smell of burning was everywhere, catching at throat and eyes. So there had been fire as well as blood, before the night's work was done. Dead men, women too, lay in a careful row across the head of the Hall, more than a score of them, brought from wherever they had fallen, and laid straight and seemly, with the warrior-patterns of their death wounds upon them.

I all but stumbled headlong over the first of them, and saw that it was young Duatha. I knew him by his thin brown hands; a boy's hands still, with the blackened thumbnail that he had jammed in a piece of chariot harness, two moons ago; not by his face, for that had been battered beyond anyone's knowing, by something heavy, a shield rim, maybe, smashed down into it again and again. Of the Escort Commander there was no sign, nor of any other Roman dead. They would have been carried off by their own kind, I supposed.

"What of the others – our own – who are not lying here?"

"Carried off for slaves. Did I not tell you? You, I am thinking they left for dead. Ah now, you will fall – let you come back and lie down."

"But you? They did not leave you for dead? –" I said foolishly. My head was full of swirling confusion, and I must stop the swirl of it and get all things straight.

"I ran and hid away; I and others also, my own People for the most part, when we knew that there was nothing we could do. At least we can be of more use to the Queen now than all her dead warriors." And she fell behind me, weeping.

The hammer was still beating in my head, but the ground was steadying somewhat beneath my feet, as I stumbled my way down the Hall, through the ashes of the hearth-fires scattered all abroad, and the overset benches. On the Dancing Floor, one of the ochre-painted skulls from the tie-beam overhead had fallen and lay grinning at me from among the mingled stains of blood and spilled wine. Something rolled under my foot, and I saw that it was an amber bead from the Queen's great necklace. And then half-hidden between an over-set table and the body of a dead hound, I caught the familiar glint of a bronze clasp on white mare's skin, and I stooped, the blood roaring like a chariot charge in my head, and heaved the dog aside, and pulled out my harp in its bag. It seems strange, now, to remember it, but for that one moment I thought of nothing more. I opened the bag and drew out my harp. It had been trodden underfoot and the strings were torn, and one horn loosened, but I knew that I could make it whole again. And for those few heartbeats of time, it seemed to me a most wonderful thing that in all that red havoc, I had my harp again; as wonderful as the sudden starry opening of a flower among the stink and filth of a knacker's yard.

The moment passed, but with its passing, much of the confusion also seemed to clear from my head. And carrying my broken harp with me, I went out through the roofless foreporch, into the Weapon Court of the Dun.

There too was the sight and smell of burning. And there, as Old Nurse had said, the warriors were gathering. Men of the Royal Clan from the outlying settlements, each with a long-hidden sword or a hurriedly furbished war-spear. And there too, standing to one side with their cloaks drawn across their faces, were their women, who had come in to be with the Queen, and to keen for the dead warriors who had no women of their own left in the Dun to keen for them.

And in the midst of her warriors, beside the tall black column of the weapon-stone, stood the Queen herself. A dead man's cloak was flung round her shoulders over her torn gown, and the royal goldwork was gone from her arms and neck, – and she carried her father's great sword, brought into the light from where ever it had lain hidden all those years; not as a man carries his sword, but cradled against her as a woman nurses a child. And behind her stood the two Princesses; but I did not look at them at all. Grief upon me, I could not. Above all, I could not look at Nessan. Coward that I am.

One of the warriors spoke up out of a long silence, as I lurched down towards them and the growing crowd parted to let me through.

"We can cut them off before they gain the border."

Boudicca cried out on him, "And then? – If we do that, more will come, and more and more, as many as the wild duck in winter, before we can make ready to receive them!"

"They will come, whether or no."

One from another, like hounds on a trail, they took up the cry.

"And what, when they come, would you have us do? Bide still and wait while they drive off the cattle and the rest of our young men, and fire the roofs over our heads?"

"Would you leave unavenged, that which they did here last night?"

The Queen looked round on them. And though she spoke no word, slowly the clamour died.

And when they were quiet again, she spoke out, swift and fierce. "Bide still and wait? Aye, we will seem to do even that, if need be, until the right time comes to unleash upon the war-trail!" There was a trickle of dried blood at the corner of her mouth, and the smudged remains of last night's eyepaint stood out livid on the grey-white of her face. "This is a greater matter than a cattle-raid and cries out for a greater revenge. So in the daylight, on the surface of things, we will bear what we must, to gain the time we need for our making ready. And in the dark beneath the daylight, we will send out by the old ways, the swift and secret ways, not only to all the Horse People, but to the tribes beyond our borders who have suffered at the Red Crests' hands or who now lie under the Red Crests' yoke, bidding them send elders and war chiefs that we may sit at the Council Fire together. Bidding them also to take their weapons from the thatch and the peat-stack, against the killing-time that comes!"

Behind her, with a sigh and a little flurry of movement, the Royal Daughter crumpled to the ground. Nessan still stood, steadying herself with one hand against the weapon-stone. Her eyes were wide and blind, and her mouth a little open as though for more air. But she was still on her feet. She had more strength than I had thought, the little dark one. The women were gathering Essylt up from her crumpled heap, carrying her away. But the Queen never even looked round.

"How long before that time comes?" someone shouted.

She lifted the great sword higher against her heart. "Not too long. My father's sword is thirsty after sleeping so long in the dark. She cries out for blood."

"*How* long before her thirst and the thirst of all our spears be quenched?" the man pressed, stubbornly.

"Two moons, maybe three, not more. The Governor of Britain, this you know, is away in the far west, making ready for war upon the Priest Kind in their chief stronghold of Môn; and our Spear Host must be gathered and ready for the war-trail before he be free again to fly his Eagles against us here in the east. Can you wait three moons, my warriors?"

A roar went up from the gathered men of the Royal Clan, and each brought his sword or spear-blade crashing down across his shield in the war salute. "We can wait three moons. Three moons, Boudicca, though our spears grow thirstier all the while!"

And Meradoc Wide-Mouth, who made laughter out of all things, cried out, "That will still leave us two to drive the Red Crests into the sea, and be home in time to gather in the harvest."

The Queen looked at him. She stood as still as the weapon-stone behind her, only her hair lifting sideways on the light sea wind, while the sudden hot clamour rose again, then died around her. And it seemed to me that she was listening, to something that no one else could hear, maybe to something far off. Maybe to something deep within herself. And when she spoke again, it was in a cool, crooning voice that stirred the hair on the back of my neck. "There shall be no harvesting in the fields of the Horse People, this year. There shall be no sowing of the seed corn, though now is the moon of sowing. This, says the All Mother, who is Lady of the Corn as well as Lady of the Foals. For since the thing that was done last night, the corn lands of the Horse People are unsacred, and shall not bear again until Red Crest blood is shed into the furrows, to give back for that which they have taken away, and purify that which they have fouled."

There was a low muttering with the sound of trouble in it, from the crowd. And then one asked, "Lady, what does the All Mother say that we shall put in our bellies when there is no grain at harvest time?"

"Fools!" said the Queen. "We shall be full fed from the Red Crests' storehouses and the rich granaries of the south!" She made a wide gesture of dismissal. "Go now. We will talk more, much more, at a later time."

And then the gathering was breaking up, the men to get their tethered horses, the remaining women, with Nessan in their midst, back to the women's quarters. I did not go with the rest. From within the shadow of the weapon-stone, where she still stood unmoving, the eyes of the Queen were upon me, their command clear as though she had spoken it. I walked towards her; and she held out one hand to me, her father's sword still in the other, and said, "Cadwan of the Harp, it is well that the Red Crests thought you dead, and more than well that they were mistaken; for what should I do without my Harper?" And, glancing at the battered bag across my shoulder, "Your harp is not scathed past the making whole again?"

"No," I said. "If I can come by the horsehair to restring her, she will sing as sweet and fierce as ever."

"There should be enough horses for that, in our runs, even now," she said. And then, "You promised that you would make me a great song one day; a song of Queen's Victories. It is in my heart that the time for you to keep that promise is almost come."

She spoke gently now, almost like the Boudicca that I have always known. But I was looking into her eyes. They were awake once more, but it was not Boudicca looking out of them; not the Boudicca that I knew at all. They were blue as ever, but the blue was only on the surface, as it might be the reflection of a clear sky, and looking into them was like looking into a dark forest, where strange and terrible things lurked half-seen among the crowding trees. And again the hair stirred on the back of my neck, and I was more afraid than ever I have been before or since. And yet, after the first shock was spent, I knew how simple it was, the thing that had happened. As a coin has two faces and yet both faces are the same coin, so it is with the Great Mother; she who gives all things in life and takes all things back in death. She is in the love of a man and a woman and the child born from it; she is in the corn that ripens to harvest, and in the seed corn that demands blood shed into the furrows before it quickens; she is in the stoop of a falcon on a leveret cowering in the long grass; she is in battle and the deaths of men. She is in all living things, even in the Queen of the Iceni who wears her godhead upon earth.

It was Boudicca looking out of those eyes still, but the other side of Boudicca, that I had never known. The dark side of the moon.

There seemed to be a wailing in the air. Maybe it was the women keening for the dead.

"I will make you your song of a Queen's Victories," I said.

I was no more afraid. Oh but the grief was on me; and I knew that the song must be a dark one, and woven for a dark Queen, however its end might be.

10

The Hosting

All that spring and into the summer, the Red Crests and the Government tribute-collectors were spread from end to end of the land, like the marsh sickness, like wolf-packs in a famine year. They say the first Romans were suckled by a she-wolf. The Procurator himself did not come again; but his orders came north from Londinium and his men were everywhere about their reivers' business. They seized the whole of Prasutagus's flocks and herds; and not his alone, for soon they were carrying off the Queen's also, and the riches of the chiefs and nobles in gold and herds and matched chariot teams; and free men and women they drove off to the slave markets. The price for murdering a Roman officer, we were told. To pay for Nero's circuses, we knew. Burning thatch and ruined farms marked their track, showing where any had dared to stand against them. And everywhere was desolation and the lowing of driven cattle, and the only things that thrived were the carrion crows. And the great officials in their purple-bordered mantles, with their bronze and crimson escorts strutted hither and yon about their ordered business of stamping a free state into part of a Roman province. And in and out among the feet of these lordly ones, like dung beetles, scurried the agents of the Roman moneylenders, calling in old debts, from men who had nothing left to pay them with but their heart's blood and an old sword hidden in the thatch.

One came to Boudicca in her ruined Hall. She was wearing a gold arm-ring that had escaped the looting of the Procurator's Escort; and she pulled it off and flung it on the ground at his feet, crying out on him, "Let you take this for surety; and for the rest, let you ask it of the Procurator, or of the Emperor himself, if he has not already spent it on wild beast shows."

And the man saw what looked out of her eyes, and bade his scribe slave take up the arm-ring and went away, promising to be back for the rest, but in a voice that shook a little.

With the Royal Dun half in ruins, and the Royal Women, so they deemed, robbed of their Royalty, the Romans left Boudicca alone, save for a visit now and then from a passing patrol, as though she were of no more account. That was the Romans' mistake, made in an ill hour.

For in the dark, beneath the surface of things, by the old secret ways, by the sunken drove-roads and the tunnelled forest tracks and the winding fen waterways, the messengers were going out, even as the Queen had said. And by the same secret ways, the chiefs and war-captains were coming in. They did not come to the Royal Dun, where the Queen abode still among the patched-up ruins of her home, lest any Roman eye should note the coming and going, but to certain forest clearings of the Priest Kind; or to a certain island among the fens, reed-fringed and alder-fringed like many others, but circled at its heart with a ring of nine ancient thorn trees.

And there, the Lady Boudicca would go to meet them. I also, most times. For where the Queen goes, there goes the Queen's Harper, that he may see and hear the things that must be passed on in song to the tribe as yet unborn.

So we would ride through the neck of the forest, and down to the black skin boats waiting among the reeds. The Queen wrapped in an old wolfskin cloak against the chill of the water-mists, and no sound as we journeyed but the stealthy lap and suckle of the water among the sedges, and somewhere a bittern booming in the night. And then we would come to the island, and go up through the reeds and the alder scrub, past the black horsehide tents pitched outside the thorn circle. There would be a fire burning at the heart of the circle, for at a Council gathering there must be light for a man to see the face of the man he speaks with; a fire of driftwood brought in from the sea coast, that its colour might not stand out too fiercely from the cold blue spirit flames that wander among those reedbeds and waterways. And around the fire, there would be the chieftains waiting; the mist catching the firelight and making a silvery smoke that swirled about their heads. About the Queen's head, too, when she put back the hood of her cloak; but no firelight seemed able to touch her eyes.

First to come were the chiefs of our own horse-runs, saying, "I can bring three hundred men, half with swords, the rest spears." – "I can bring six score men to the Hosting, and fourteen chariots, each with a fighting man beside the driver." – "I have four hundred and a handful, young braves, who have taken to the forest to be out of the Red Crests' path until I call them forth, but for the most part no arms save hunting-spears and slings. . . ."

And then came chiefs from further off; foremost among them, leaders of the Trinovantes hot for

Roman blood to wipe out years of bondage. "Eighteen years," said Vortrix the Bear, acting as spokesman for the rest, "eighteen years, we have been treated by the Romans as a conquered people. Our Royal Dun – for remember, Lady, that Dun Camulus was ours before the Catuvellauni set up their High Place there – our Royal Dun they have crushed down beneath a Roman city that has stolen even its name; a city with Roman baths and theatres and circuses, and a great temple to their Emperor Claudius. And in the temple, we, the chiefs and nobles of the Trinovantes, and our women with us must take our turns to serve as priests and priestesses to this Emperor God who is not ours, so that our own gods turn their faces from us – because, forsooth, that is the way of the great men and the noble ladies in Rome! And we must pay out of our own dwindling store-kists for the festivals in the temple and the plays in the theatre and the games in the circus, when ever our masters call for them, while at the same time our land is stripped from us and handed over to Roman settlers, and our lesser folk are set to working for those same settlers – old Red Crests who treat all men not of their own kind as slaves."

"That is a tale all men know," said the Queen when he had grumbled on long enough, like the bear of his name. "Tell me now, what fighting strength you can yet raise?"

And he spoke the number, in horsemen and foot-spears and chariot-warriors. And the Oak Priest who kept the tally wrote them all down on his peeled willow-rods. And when that was done, Vortrix said, "There is another thing that we can give to the strength of the War Host, though it may not be numbered in the tally."

"What thing is that?" said the Queen.

"Men, women too within the city, who are no friends to Rome, who can tell of evil omens, and set unchancy whispers running, and spread confusion in men's minds."

And the Queen smiled. "A few such men within an enemy stronghold may be worth many chariots outside the gates. We will talk more of this at another time."

From the Coritani of the mid-country to our west, chiefs came; and from the Cornovi, whose runs are towards the high hills westward of that again. The Chariot Lords of the Parisi, and Princes of the Brigantes from over beyond Ostorius Scapula's old frontier, the Bearers of the Blue War-shields, proudest of the proud.

Captains of the Catuvellauni too, promising war-bands. Aye, war-bands from the Cats of War, who had counted themselves Lords of the World, and our enemies, before the Romans came! Boudicca looked at them when they stood before her; and the memory was in us all, of old menace and old border raids, of how they had slain the King her father, and how we had taken the friendship oath with Rome, that the Roman yoke might be the more surely clamped upon their necks. And the Catuvellauni and the Brigantes looked at each other, remembering that when Caratacus had gone for refuge to the Brigantian Queen, she had handed him over for a gift to Rome.

So many memories lying dark behind men's eyes. And I thought, "This is a team that will take some driving." And I looked at Boudicca in her wolfskin cloak, with her father's sword in her hands, and the sea-coloured firelight shining in her hair but never reaching her eyes; and I thought "But this is the driver who can handle them if any can."

Men came and went again; and the Council Fires burned in the nights. And by chains of watchers and riders all across the tribes between, came word of Suetonius Paulinus the Governor, with his legions on the far western coast, making ready for his attack on Môn. We must unleash our own attack before he was done, with his and his hands free once more; yet we must wait as far as we could into the summer, that there might be grass enough for the horses, so many horses all together. And the rising, when it came, must be swift, with small time for Hosting beforehand, to give warning to our enemies of what was to come.

So the war-pattern was worked out, for secrecy at the start of things, and speed when the time came. And all the while as the curlew came up from the marshes to nest on the higher ground, and lambing time came and went, and the mares dropped their foals, and the whitethorn flowered and scattered its petals to the wind, men took their bird-bows into the marshes, hunting the heron for their hackle feathers to furbish long-hidden war-spears, and old swords were brought out, aye, mine among them, from their hiding places. And in secret clearings in the oak woods, where the best of the horses had been hidden already, and the best of the warriors, too, the smiths and armourers mended old weapons and forged new ones; and new war-chariots were built, and hunting chariots strengthened with dappled oxhides lashed over their wicker sides; and the great wagons for the baggage and the women and the children who could not be left behind. We had never had baggage wagons before. The Romans, but not us. But we had not fought this kind of war before; and now we should need them.

Through all the lands of the Horse People, it seemed to me, was a quivering in the air, a low muttering in the ground itself, a menacing hum like the distant voice of swarming bees. But the Red Crests, strutting to and fro in the daylight, did not hear what sounded in the dark beneath their feet. Even the cornland lying brown and fallow, that should have been green with springing barley told them nothing, for they thought their harrying had made us overpass this year's seed time. No more.

And I, I made a new wolfskin sheath for my sword, and when that was done, I mended my harp and restrung it, and made for it a fresh bag of well-cured mare's skin. And there were evenings when the day's spear practice was over, when Nessan would leave her sister to polishing and repolishing her blade, and come to be with me, as I coaxed the wracked frame back into shape, and twisted the horsehair for new strings. But she never sang any more, and when the mending was done, and I would have had her to pluck the strings (there is no other, even her mother, who I would have let to touch them) she shook her head. "There is no music in me, any more. I lost it along with the rest. I could never be a Queen's Harper now."

And my heart wept blood for her, and I would have given my own gift of song to have my hands round the throat of the man who had driven hers away. And I snapped the twisted horsehair under my fingers, cutting my hand so that the red sprang out in a thin line.

That was within a moon of midsummer, when the nights grow short, and after sunset the light lingers in the north like the echo of the sea in a shell, until it turns toward sunrise again. And before midsummer, two things came to pass at the same time. The watchers in the west sent word that Suetonius Paulinus had had his victory against Môn and was already making to leave his war-camp beyond the mountains and march his legions back to the great base fortress they call Glevum. That was the one thing; and for the other: the Red Crests who came each year about that time for their muster of young men for the auxiliaries, came again, just as though it were last year or any year before that, but demanding a greater number because we were part of the Province, and no longer a free state.

But we had other need of our young braves. And the grass was tall enough for grazing the horses. So then we knew that the time was come to be sending out the Cran-Tara.

The hazel tree was felled; and rods cut from it, as many as were needed. And while one end of each rod was charred in the fire, the black goat was brought for slaying, to the threshold of the Hall, where the Queen stood waiting with a long knife in her hand, that caught and mingled the red of the fire and the white of the young moon on its blade. Two men dragged it forward by the horns, bleating wildly, for it smelled its own death. But when it was close before her, Boudicca bent forward and set her empty hand on its forehead between the horns, and spoke softly, looking into its eyes; and the bleating stopped. Then she cut its throat. Blood spurted out over her hand. She looked at her hand and smiled; the first time that I had seen her smile in many moons; and drew her hand across her forehead, leaving a great dark smear behind, and touched her cheeks and even her lips with her fingers. Then while the goat still lay twitching, she took the hazel rods and dipped the uncharred end of each into the hole in its throat, and gave each to the man waiting for it.

So the Cran-Tara went out; the summons that speaks of death by fire and sword.

And that night, every Roman in Icenian territory died. That would give us silence for a few days. And before the Romans beyond our borders began to wonder, and think of sending to ask questions, we should have no more need of silence.

Before dawn, the first and nearest of the war-bands had come in.

For three days the Hosting went on. On foot and on horseback and behind their chariot teams, the warriors came in, leading spare horses but half-broken, even mares whose foals had been killed to set them free for war. Men bearing old weapons or new ones hastily forged in those forest clearings, the war-patterns already daubed red and yellow on their cheeks and foreheads. Women, too, and boys not yet come to manhood, carrying their fathers' heaviest hunting-spears.

The Royal Dun became the centre of a vast camp, and the horses grazed under guard all across the countryside; and the smoke of a hundred cooking-fires rose on the evening air. And men brought their swords to the tall black stone in the Weapon Court to whet the blades that were already keen beyond any need of whetting. And at dusk, when the light of the cooking-fires brightened from red to gold, the young braves made their war dances, whirling and crouching and leaping to the rhythm of their own stamping heels and the clash of spear on shield and the throbbing of the wolfskin drums. And in the secret places of the forest, the Priest Kind wove their own hidden ceremonies for victory.

And on the second day came the Parisi, their chariot columns raising a summer dust-storm behind them; and watching them come, I was thinking that Prasutagus would have been proud of his kindred.

And throughout the third day and far into that night, in small bands already drunk with the promise of war, came the Brigantes, with their blue painted war-shields and their great spears crying out for blood.

Then the first part of the Hosting was complete. And at daybreak, with a great braying and booming of horns, we swept south on the war trail.

Boudicca led the swarm in her chariot covered with red and white bulls' hides; the horses of her team bay-coloured, and so dark that there seemed a bloom on their hides like the bloom on a thunder-cloud. And for driver, Brockmail who had been Prasutagus's charioteer. Her hair was bound back in a single braid thicker than a warrior's wrist, to keep it out of her way, but her cloak, a warrior's cloak, flowed back from her, red as flame on the wind of our going. And we followed the flame-flicker of that cloak, more than the stallion-skull standard with its streaming saffron tassels that a mounted chieftain carried beside her.

And when I looked back from my place among the warriors close about her, I saw the War Host like a bee-swarm following the Queen, a dark spreading stain of men and beasts and thundering wheels reaching back and back towards the lumbering ox-wagons of the rear, where the Princesses rode with the

Queen's women in the great Royal Wagon with its high roof of painted and tasselled horsehides. But I could not see the wagons, they were so far behind, and the summer dust-cloud rising and thickening over all.

And I felt the slap of my old sword against my thigh. And I felt the harp in her bag behind my shoulder stir in her sleep, ready to wake and sing. Hush, my harp, for the time is not yet, for singing; and bright dark and terrible the song will be.

To the Lady Julia Procilla, at the House of the Three Walnut Trees in Massilia, Province of Southern Gaul. From Tribune Gneus Julius Agricola, on the Staff of the Governor of Britain. Greeting.

Dearest and most honoured Mother, I grow doubtful as to whether any of my letters written from our forward base camp at Segontium will have reached you. All things are somewhat uncertain here, including the post. Therefore I make brief repeat of what was in them.

I reported for duty here at Deva, to find the Governor just about to march with the Twentieth and part of the Fourteenth Legions in to the far west, to subdue the native priesthood who are the heart and core of tribal resistance to our rule, and who had withdrawn into their last stronghold, the Island of Môn, off the mountainous west coast of this Province. Môn, it seems, is also the chief granary of much of western Britain and therefore better under our control. We were away something over three months, chiefly spent in building our base camp between the mountains and the sea, and making ready such boats and rafts as we could for the crossing. Mother, you should have seen that crossing! The boats served for those who could not get over in any other way, but the rest of us had to swim for it. To be sure, the Straits are only a mile wide, but the current runs fast there. The Friezian auxiliaries made the best showing, being mighty swimmers and well used to estuary work in their own land; and they formed the vanguard. The cavalry came next, each man fully armed and swimming beside his horse; the Staff also, which of course included me and Felix, who is reputedly the ugliest horse in three legions, but has a heart to match Bukephalus. (Come to think of it, with a name like that, Bukephalus was probably ugly, too.) And to his everlasting credit, the Governor himself. Paulinus is a hard man; not much mercy in him, I think; but he never asks any of his men to do what he will not do himself. Therefore there is little grumbling among the ranks who serve under him.

Well, we made the crossing, stirred up our hornets' nest, and met a great, and I must say valiant resistance, with heavy fighting on the landing beach. The warriors in a kind of frenzy, almost as though they had taken aconite or the like, cried on by the Druids, many of whom fought among them. Dark-robed furies who seemed to be women, too. It isn't good, finding a woman at your throat, and knowing you have to kill her or she will kill you. I know, I've done it. I wonder if I'll ever make a soldier. Anyhow, we finished the job, wiped out the Druid stronghold and hacked down the sacred groves, and left Môn desolate and full of dead behind us. Paulinus says it's like cauterizing a sore or burning out a hornets' nest. And here we are back in Deva.

There were no letters waiting for me here, which is what chiefly makes me wonder if you have received mine. The posts, as I say, are very uncertain, and everybody is looking anxiously for letters from home.

The trumpet has just sounded for watch-changing, and I am on duty. It is good for one's self-esteem to be chosen by the Governor for his Tenting Companion, but of all posts on the Staff, it leaves one less time to oneself than almost anybody else in the fort.

I'll finish this later.

Later: In haste. Word has just come in of some kind of rising in the east of the Province, headed by the Iceni. Paulinus has determined to ride for Londinium and his supply base tomorrow, leaving the legions and other foot to follow, all that can be spared from garrison-duty and frontier work. (It will take them the best part of a week, even forced marching, and the gods know what can happen in a week. Hence his decision that the cavalry push ahead.) Also he has sent a galloper to summon the Second from Glevum to join us. I am of course leaving Marcipor here. He begs me to tell you that it is not *his* fault if my things are not properly looked after.

I have a chance to send this off with the official despatches, and Jupiter alone knows when I shall have such a chance again.

Your dutiful and affectionate son
Gneus Julius Agricola

11

The Grove of the Mother

Five days the War Host swept southward. Four nights we camped beside the way; and all the while we gathered strength and power as the war-bands of other tribes came in to join us at the appointed Hosting places along the way; and they leaving all the land westward up in arms behind them. The Trinovantes and the Cats of War joined us last of all, some on their own borders, less than a day from Dun Camulus, some within sight of the city. And the Trinovantes brought with them wild stories of omens and portents, voices crying woe in the empty theatre, the statue of Victory in the temple fallen from its place with its back towards our advance as though it sought to flee, and all within the city lost in fear and confusion.

"Truly," said the Queen, "did I not say that five men in the heart of an enemy stronghold are worth many chariots outside the gates."

Though indeed there were no gates. No gates, no walls, for such defences are not allowed to Roman provincial cities. The people of Camulodunum must have felt the mistake of that, in the past few days, since they had known of the tempest sweeping down upon them from the north. They had sent to Londinium for help, said Vortrix the Bear. But the Procurator had sent them only some two hundred men, ill-armed and slack trained, from the depot garrison, who had reached them scarcely a full day ahead of us. They had made some attempt to throw up rough barricades across the main streets. But it is in my mind that they must have thought with longing of the great turf banks that walled the Royal Dun in King Togodumnos's day.

The outlying farms and steadings were empty, for their slaves had joined us or melted away, and their owners had fled to the little safety the city could give them. We slaughtered abandoned cattle and drove off the horses, and fired the buildings as we went by. But not all were quite deserted. In one of the first, we found a man; old and sick. Maybe he had stayed of his own will, maybe he had been abandoned there. But I think he was the master of the house. And he stood clinging to the doorpost for support, and watched us come. In his free hand he held a short Roman sword, but when he would have lifted it, it fell from his grasp.

Boudicca had bidden her charioteer to pull aside there, because there was a well under a cherry-tree in the open courtyard, and she was thirsty. And when he reined up, she stood looking down at the man in the doorway, while the team fidgeted for their heads. And he stood looking back at her, his empty sword hand fumbling a little as though he half thought to feel the hilt still in it.

"Poor old man," she said. "Could your people not even wait to give you the mercy-stroke before they fled? Then we must do it for them." And she made a gesture with her hand to the warriors gathered round; and they cut him down, quite cleanly and quickly.

"He was a brave old man," said the Queen. "And he deserved that. But it is the last mercy that we show until the wrath of the Mother is washed away with blood, and the Tribes are free once more. Let you strike off his head."

So they hacked off his head. But his grey hair was cut short in the Roman fashion. Too short for tying to a chariot rim. So the young braves stuck it on a spear, to carry among the standards. And somebody took a brand that still smouldered on the hearth, and fired the thatch. And when the Queen had had her drink from the well under the cherry-tree, we crashed on to regain the head of the War Host.

The ground sloped down to the river; and on the far side we saw the city on its low whale-backed hill, the evening sunlight on the white and red and gold of the great temple in its midst. The people of the city had hacked down the bridge; but that made small difference; it would have taken too long to get a War Host across one narrow bridge, and that within javelin throw of the nearest buildings on the city slopes. We swung off righthandwise and forded the river at low tide further up; and that night we made our camp among the ruined banks of the old Dun, westward of the new city, where, eighteen years before, I had come, riding behind Prasutagus, when the Kings gathered to swear faith and friendship with the Emperor Claudius in King Togodumnos's High Hall. You could not even see where the Hall had been now, its stones and timbers had gone with all else that was of use from the great Dun, to help build the new city of Camulodunum. I knew where it had been by an ancient yew tree that had grown in the forecourt. Maybe it was sacred; for some reason or none, they had left it alone. For me, it was a landmark, but I did not speak of it to the Queen.

They made the wagon-park where the elephant lines had been, that other time. And when the dusk came down their great humped outlines against the sky brought past things very near. And dead men, too; dead men, too.

The Queen did not sleep with the Princesses and her women in the Royal Wagon; but as she had slept every night since the setting out, between the wheels of her chariot, her warriors sleeping on their spears around her, and she lying with her cheek on her father's sword.

There was a restlessness in the air; comings and goings between the watchfires, ponies stamping and fidgeting as though they smelled tomorrow's wind. Faint sounds from the city, awake and restless also; waiting as we were waiting. I could not sleep. I went and walked in a little wood in the loop of the river below the camp. A small wood, but a dark one, of ancient trees, oak and yew. A little earlier in the year I might have thought to hear the nightingale as I passed in among the first of the trees. But the further in I went the more it seemed to me that no bird would ever sing in that wood. Silence held it; silence that hung like mist among the trees, allowing not even a rustle among the undergrowth, and I found myself moving with care not to break it. The Grove of the Mother, the Trinovantes call it, a sacred wood. And suddenly it came to me that the whole wood was waiting; waiting for something that was not mine to see; and also that I was not alone in it. And I would have turned back, but in the same moment, I came upon the edge of a small clearing, where the moonlight plashed through the branches onto a circle of open turf; soft short turf for a dancing floor, among the crowding trees.

And then I knew why I had felt that I was not alone. For in the centre of the clearing, the red of her cloak quenched almost to black by the moonlight, stood

Boudicca, who I had thought asleep between the wheels of her chariot. Tree-tall and straight and still, her arms stretched wide to the moon in an agony, an ecstasy of prayer.

I froze among the trees, like an animal when it scents danger. And she dropped the cloak from her shoulders. And under it she was naked. And naked, she began to dance, treading a circle of strange small steps round and round; and as she danced, her head tipped far back, she drew her hands again and again down her breasts; gently, it seemed, almost as though she caressed herself; but behind each stroking movement, the track of her fingernails showed dark on her white skin, like the claw marks of a cat. A low crooning came from her; and I knew that the web she wove was one of those that are not for a man's watching. And I covered my eyes and crouched back into the deepest shadow, and stole away, having more care than ever, not to break the silence.

When the horns sounded at first light to rouse the camp, the Queen rose from where she seemed to have slept all night between the wheels of her chariot with her bodyguard about her. And the wild beast marks were hidden beneath the bright checkered stuff of her gown; and almost, I wondered if I had been dreaming.

Men ate the morning barley cake while they harnessed up the chariot teams that had been picketed close all night. And the sun had not yet cleared the rim of the world to touch the proud roofs of Camulodunum, when the war-horns began snarling for the attack.

We were half round the city, covering the two sides that were not held by the river; and certain war-bands thrust forward between the city and the riverbanks to omplete the circle and swarm up from the shipping uays. But we thrust in our main attack along the road ridge that made level going from the old Dun. he Princesses had been left with the other women nd the children and the Priest Kind among the agons. But the Queen's chariot led the foremost olumn. Her war-captains had sought to make her ait in safety, but she said, "The Mother will let no arm come to me until it is time. I am the spear in her and; I am the people's freedom. How shall the war- iors follow me if I do not lead?" And so again we ollowed the red flame-lick of her cloak. Again I rode lose behind her chariot, among the horse warriors of er bodyguard; and among us also, behind the tandard-bearer, rode one carrying aloft on its spear- haft the head of the old man we had killed yesterday. Morning sun under a low sky caught the sour-white orse-skull and streaming saffron tassels of the stan- dards; and the ground shivered under our hooves and vheels, and the dust-cloud rose, and the clods flew back from our horses' hooves.

And so we crashed in through the sunken wreck of old earthworks, and between the first neat white houses of the city fringes, giving tongue like the Wild Hunt, to crash into the first barricades, the first lines of hose gathered to defend the place against us.

But save for the Queen and her following column, we did not carry the chariot charge beyond the city boundaries, for the narrow gullies made by the streets would not serve for chariot warfare. So after the first shock, the first crumbling of the outer barricades, while the horsemen thrust on, the charioteers reined back according to custom, and the chariot warriors eapt down and rushed ahead on foot.

And then we found that the men of Camulodunum who were fools and tyrants, were not also cowards They met us, old men and boys in greasy leathe tunics, with short Roman swords in their hands, an fought us for every street corner, every garden wal and shop doorway, every spear's-length of the way We were glad, for it is not good to fight cowards; it set no fire to the blood.

There was fire enough in our blood, that day!

I took little part in the fighting. A harper is not warrior. But no man should go into battle leaving it t other men who have work of their own to do, t protect him. I had my old sword, and I used it whe need arose, and found that my hand had no altogether lost its cunning.

All day we fought them slowly back, while the rushed us down every side-street and made of ever building a fortress; back and back from one barricad of piled grain-sacks and upturned carts to the next until our feet slipped in the red gutters, and the dea lay piled at every corner. Their dead and ours tumble together, but they had no more living to take the plac of those that fell. . . .

Even so, in narrow ways four men may hold bac many, and the day was close to noon before we weclear the outer quarters of the city and thrust on towards th fine tall buildings and open spaces at the heart. An always, in the forefront of the fighting, we followe the red flame-lick of the Queen's warrior cloak and he bright hair.

By sunset, the city was ours. A wild, fiery sunse half lost behind drifting smoke, for in half a score o places, Camulodunum was burning – and most of th defenders yet alive had fallen back on the great templ o the Divine Claudius and made their stronghold here.

All next day, while we flung in attack after attack, hey held the temple against us. It was good to have an nemy worth the killing. It was dusk when they made heir last stand. But the dusk was swallowed up in the urnace-glare of burning Camulodunum; and the teps were slippery with blood and filth, and the white olumns splashed with it. They stood shoulder braced gainst shoulder, and I saw the light of the flames in heir eyes; and they did not give back any further, for here was no further to go, but died where they stood; he old men and the boys in their worn leather tunics nd battered armour. I have held a warmer heart for he Roman kind since that night than ever I held efore.

The War Host was drunk with bloodshed as well as wine from the wine-shops that they had broken into, nd with vengeance and with victory. There were women and children packed close in the inner part of he temple; some still living, though many of the women had killed their children and then let out their own lives before the warriors broke in. The still living children they hacked down and were done with quickly. But the Queen had ordered that all captive women were to be brought to her. So they gathered up he women – the screaming, terrified, foolish women – who had not had the sense or the courage to kill hemselves while there was yet time, and brought them to the Queen, where she stood in her chariot behind her tired team, in the open space that the Romans call the Forum, clear of the rags of fire dropping from the burning city.

Some of them were young and fair. I saw them.

They fell on their knees, crying out to her for mercy, because she was a woman like themselves. She looked down at them. And as the light of the Council Fires had never reached the darkness within her eyes, nor did the flames of burning Camulodunum. And she bade the men who held the captives take them to the Grove of the Mother, outside the town; and she sent back word for the women who waited with the wagon train to come to her there. And word also for three chiefs from every tribe of the War Host; which was a strange thing indeed. . . .

I will not tell, I will not remember, how they died, those women. But after all was over, I saw their bodies hanging there, like dreadful white fruit hanging from the branches of the dark and ancient trees, and I knew what Boudicca had promised to the Great Mother when I saw her dancing there, two nights ago. And I knew why the wood had grown full of fear.

To the Lady Julia Procilla, in the House of the Three Walnut Trees at Massilia, Province of Southern Gaul. From Gneus Julius Agricola, outside Londinium.

Greetings, my Mother. I have no means of knowing how, or when – or if – I shall be able to send this off to you. The whole country is seething like yeast beside the fire. And at least in the part of the Province that we have covered in the past few days, the official Government despatch riders have either been killed or run for it. The whole road from Deva has made cheerless riding; mostly through "sub hostile" territory, which is to say that the tribes would have come for us if they could, but most of their best warriors are out with the Iceni. We have had a few arrows out of the woods; one horse killed and a couple of troopers wounded. But for the most part we seemed to be riding through an empty desolation; the posting stations burned out, and the odd corpse in the ditch along the way. They have cut the road more than a day's march from Londinium; simply uprooted it and left raw ground and felled trees across where it used to be. So not caring to ride straight into an ambush, we cast round to the south, forded the Thamesis and finally came up on the city from the south side. The gods alone know if the legions will get through behind us. Anyhow, Paulinus has sent in messengers and we enter Londinium tomorrow.

Before we had to leave the road, we got word from Lindum that Petilius Cerialis was heading south with a vexhilation of the Ninth Legion, two thousand strong, in an attempt to save Camulodunum, which lies directly in the path the rebels are taking. But there seems little chance of his getting there in time to head them off. Probably the town has already fallen. Now, we hear nothing. Paulinus says that is always the way of it when you get close in to the heart of things – like being in the heart of a dust-storm. Everything shuts down.

12

The Washer by the Ford

From the first, on the word of Gretorix Hard-Council and his kind, it had been determined that when we had dealt with Camulodunum across our path, we should thrust straight on for Londinium and the supply base there; the only place where we could come by all the weapons and war-gear that we needed, without having to waste time in storming Roman forts to get them. That made good sense to the head; also Londinium was the place of officials and money-lenders and fat merchants, and the tribesmen who had become lap-dogs of Rome. And that made good sense of another kind, to the heart. But before we could head for Londinium, there must be a day or more for seeing to our wounded and burying our dead. And while that was still in the doing, and while parts of Camulodunum still burned, and the warriors were still questing like hounds through the smoking ruins after food and gold and gear, anything that had escaped the fire and yet remained, it was found that the three war-bands of the Brigantes and a scattering of men from the Coritani and Cornovi, having gathered all that they could carry, had taken their horses and melted away in the night.

When the word was brought to Boudicca the Queen, she called her chiefs and war-captains together, and said to them, "It has been told to me that certain men of the War Host have stolen away without leave taking. Therefore I would have you tell me the meaning of this. Speak first, Tigernann of the Brigantes, since most of them are of your following."

And Tigernann of the Brigantes, who was a prince in his own right, stood swinging to and fro on the balls of his feet with his thumbs stuck in his belt, and said, "It is the custom of the war-trail. The raid is finished and the spoils are gathered and the warriors are away home."

"You also? And the rest of your following?" said the Queen.

"Not yet. Londinium should be worth the sacking. But we are no vassals of yours, Lady, when we choose to go, we shall go."

"That was not how it was agreed round the Council Fire," said the Queen. "You speak to me the customs of the cattle raid; but this is no cattle raid. Are you grown witless that you do not understand? If we scatter and go streaming home with a few gold cups before we have driven the Red Crests into the sea, none of us will ever be free of them! Nor will the Mother forgive me if we turn back from the full vengeance that she demands!"

"As to the vengeance, that is for you to take, go you and take it," said Tigernann. "As to the freedom – we have freedom enough beyond the frontier, while we have our hills and our high moors and our peat bogs among which the Red Crests do not know their way. We will join with you in tearing Londinium to rags, if it pleases us, or we will go home now, if that pleases us better." He grinned. "Or it may even be that we will go and offer our spears to the Red Crests, for I am thinking that they will be grateful for every spear-arm that they can get just now."

"Grateful enough to forget the sacking of a Roman city?" said Boudicca, and her lips lifted back from her teeth. "Or do you think they will not know whose standard you have followed in these past days? Fools! From this trail, there can be no turning back!"

There was a low, angry muttering, and men looked to and fro among each other, while the chiefs of the Iceni pulled in closer about the Queen. But before Tigernann could answer her, Andragius of the Catuvellauni spoke up, gentling his left wrist that was bound with bloody rags.

"Assuredly, from this trail there can be no turning back." And he swung round from one to another of the war-captains behind Tigernann, lashing them as with a whip of savage laughter. "Oh you witless ones! Do you not know why she did the thing that she did two nights since in the Grove of the Mother? Nor why she called in chiefs from every tribe of the War Host, to have a part in it? Do you think the Romans will ever forget *that*?"

There was a long, jagged silence. Beyond the silence were the sounds of the war-camp, voices and the ring of the armourer's hammer, the neigh of a horse, the lowing of captured cattle driven in for slaughter. But within the circle of the war-captains, only the silence. Then Tigernann looked round at his fellows, and shrugged. "Nay now, I did but jest. As to those who have gone – there are those in every War Host who will go their own way, and the War Host is the better without them."

And the moment passed.

I looked at the Queen. Her eyes were opened wide, and for the first time in a long while, something looked out of them. I thought that it was horror. Then she turned, and dropping the whole company behind her like a fouled cloak, walked away.

Before noon, one of our hunter scouts rode into camp on a blown horse, with word that nearly half of the Ninth Legion were less than a day's march away, coming down on us from Lindum. But we had known that they must be on our track within a day or so, and the plan was already made.

Some seven Roman miles upstream from Camulodunum, the new legions' road that runs straight as a spear-shaft north-west to Lindum, crosses the river by a paved ford. Forest and scrub country all thereabouts; good country for an ambush. Before the noon sun had moved a handspan over to the westward, Andragius, with the Cats of War, and a strong band of the Trinovantes, who best knew their own countryside, were on their way. . . .

The day passed. And Boudicca was no more seen, but when the smoke rose from the cooking-fires to mingle with the darker smell of burning that still drifted from the silent town, and the lights and shadows lay long across the land, she came out from the Royal Wagon and fell to ranging about the camp. And as the sun sank lower and the high grey sky drifting up before the summer wind began to flush with shadowy foxglove colours, it seemed that the whole great camp was not big enough for her restlessness.

Then she called for me, and with the warriors of her bodyguard following a little behind, she wandered down to the river, and so came to the place where the War Host had forded it four days ago. The banks were torn down for a spear-throw up and down stream. The foxglove pink was deepening to furnace red in the west, and the river running out on the ebb tide caught the same colour, running flame-streaked between shadowy alder-fringed banks.

The Queen checked in her walking, and stood looking down into the eddies. "The water is running red."

I thought of that other ford, seven Roman miles up river. "It is only the sunset in the water," I said.

She shook her head. "The Washer by the Ford is washing blood-stained clothes, do you not see her?"

The evening wind seemed suddenly chill between my shoulders, and I looked where she was looking. But there was only an old alder tree trailing its hair in the water.

"There is no one there," I told her. "You speak foolishness because you are weary. But you must not let the War Host hear such foolishness."

"You think that they would take fear, and yet more of them melt away?" she said drearily. And then she asked, "Was it true, the thing that Andragius of the War Cats said, that none of them can turn back because of the offering we made together in the Grove of the Mother?"

"I think so, yes. But even though they will not melt away, such ill-omened talk as that may suck the heart out of them and leave it cold."

I do not think she even heard that part. She said, "Cadwan of the Harp, is it true, as he said, that that is why I made the offering?"

And at first I could not answer. I remembered her dancing naked to the moon in that Grove, and I knew that it was not. But I remembered also, how she had called in chiefs from every tribe that rode with us, to take a part in the horror, even though it was so much a matter of the Women's Side that she had not called for the Priests. I remembered further back, the bare fields where she had ordered no corn to be sown; and along with that memory, stories I had heard from traders and the like, of Red Crest leaders, who, landing on an enemy shore, had burned their own ships behind them, that there might be no way back, and no way open ahead but victory.

"Is it true?" she demanded again, urgently.

And I said, "Few of us know the full truth of our own hearts."

"But the All Mother knows . . . It is needful for the War Host to be bound together. Yet if I have misused the Priest-Power, if I have bent my vow to her so that it serves another purpose, then her wrath is upon me, and it will be for me and all who follow me that she washes bloody linen by the ford." And she gripped her hands together, driving them against her teeth until the knuckles broke and bled. Then she said again, wailingly, "But the War Host must be bound together, or how can the evil be washed away. How can we ever be free again?"

And how could I answer her? It was a raven that answered, flying over from the smoking ruins of Camulodunum, black-winged against the flaming bars of the sunset. It croaked as though in harsh mockery, and Boudicca raised her head and listened.

For a little, it had seemed that something human, maybe even the Boudicca I knew, had been there. But sudden as a priest putting on a god-head, that Boudicca was lost again, and the other was back, with only the forest darkness looking out of her eyes. "I am what I am," she said. "I do what I do. Now I would drink, for the thirst is on me."

And going back, I took the horned war-cap from one

of the bodyguard, and brought her water from among the alder roots; and she took it from me and drank deep, the sunset reflecting red as blood in the helmet-cup.

In the short clear darkness of the summer night, the war-bands returned, they carried fringed and coloured standards with gilt laurel wreaths on them; and when Boudicca came out from her sleeping place to meet them, they tumbled Roman heads at her feet.

"The cavalry wing escaped," the Prince Andragius told her. "Their Legate with them. Some of our warriors are away after them yet."

"But the rest?" said the Queen.

"They died well," Andragius said. "So we brought you the heads of their captains, for they were worth the taking."

She looked down at the heads in the light of the nearest watchfire. Dawn was not far off, and somewhere down towards the river, a willow-wren had begun singing. "I saw their deaths in the river at sunset," she said.

Mother, we have been in Londinium two days, and it seems that tomorrow we pull out again. The place is not really defensible, unwalled and straggling. Only the supply base is entrenched and palisaded, and has a small garrison – very small; our valiant Procurator sent half of it up to hold Camulodunum against the rebels, before he himself hurried aboard the last ship to leave for Gaul. It seems to have been largely his treatment of the Iceni that fired the heather in the first place.

When we rode in, the people here greeted us as saviours; and Paulinus did have some idea that if we got everyone herded into the supply depot, and the Second Legion did get through to us from Glevum, we could hold out, with them and our own cavalry and the remains of the garrison, plus every able-bodied male we could arm with a spear, until the Twentieth and the Fourteenth arrived.

But it hasn't worked out like that.

The Second has let us down – at least their camp Commandant has. The Legate is away, and he (the C.C.) has refused the Governor's summons, on the grounds that if he strips Glevum of its troops, revolt may flare in the south-west. The galloper got back to us with that word this morning – by the southern road, clear of all the trouble. Paulinus has sent back repeating the order, but it will be too late now, anyway. The tribes have sacked and burned Camulodunum, and it looks as though they have ambushed and wiped out the vexhilation of the Ninth somewhere. No direct news as to that, but reliable reports of the cohort standards having been seen in rebel hands. And now the rebels are thrusting south again. The Iceni seem to have gathered to themselves war-bands from all over the north and west of the Province, and the whole pack of them led by their Queen, Prasutagus's widow (I begin to see why we have always looked on the Furies as women!).

The merchants plead for us to stay and defend them; but the situation is hopeless, and to remain here in Londinium, would be to allow ourselves to be trapped, and waste what troops we have to no purpose. So Paulinus has given the order to pull out tomorrow, by the south-west road towards Noviomagus. That's really the only road that's open to us. We shall be pulling back into friendly territory, King Cogidubnos of the Regni being our staunchest ally. Maybe he will even be able to gather us some fighting men; we're like to need every man we can get, even if the legions get through to us; the Governor is even taking the remains of the depot garrison. He has made it known that we will take with us any refugees who choose to come and are strong enough to make the march. But we cannot take the old or the sick or children; and that must mean that few women will be free to come with us, and that many of the men will elect to remain. For them, the depot is being opened and arms issued. I suppose if you are going to die it is better to go down with a spear in your hand than stand to be butchered like sheep.

Some people are taking to the country southward, though I do not think they will find much safety there. A donkey is fetching more than a matched chariot team would have done a week ago. The bridge is being kept clear for the troops, and anyone who owns a boat is making a fortune this evening. Only gold isn't much good to you when you are dead. You can imagine the scene in the streets. If I were Governor of Britain, I wonder if I'd have the courage to pull out and leave this place to its fate. I hope I should, because it's the only thing to do. But I'm not at all sure I should – have the courage, I mean.

Paulinus is shouting for me. I'll try to add to this from time to time, in case the chance ever comes to send it off to you.

I do not need to ask you to think of me when you go each evening to our little household shrine.

13

Londinium

We left Camulodunum with the ravens gathered over its blackened ruins, hanging and swirling like fragments of charred thatch in a high wind.

Our best hunters who were the Eyes and Ears of the War Host far ahead, had sent back word that Suetonius Paulinus was in Londinium, but no more than a few squadrons of cavalry with him, while the two legions he had brought back from Môn were on the march from the great fortress of Deva to join him. So from Camulodunum we went two ways, Andragius with the Catuvellauni and upward of half the War Host taking the road for Verulamium to cut off the legions on their march and deal with them as they had dealt with the Ninth, while the other half pressed on straight for Londinium, following again the scarlet flame of the Queen's mantle, and bearing with us in triumph the coloured and gilded standards of the Red Crest cohorts. Captured Roman weapons also, we had now, to add to our own. Not much of armour; it is in my mind that a man must be trained to it before he can move easily in the heavy Roman war-gear. But here and there among us was a leather tunic or the russet of a soldier's cloak or the crimson hackle of a helmet crest; and there was Roman grain and wine and gold necklaces and cooking-pots in the wagons that brought up our rear.

So we flowed south like a river in spate for three

days, until slowly the country changed and the made road left the flat lands and the willows and the alder woods and climbed into the higher ground and great dark forest stretches of oak and beech and yew that circle Londinium to the north.

And on the evening of the third day, our wagons left far behind us, we came over a long hill-crest, and looked out from the woodshore over scrubland that sank away to corn and pasture, and saw far away to the south through the summer haze, a great sprawling town beside a broad river. And the town might almost have been a cloud shadow, but the evening light touched the water and we knew it for the Father of Rivers.

We camped that night on the woodshore. They must have seen our watchfires strung out along the high ground. And to us in the darkness before dawn, came one who looked like a smith – like enough he was a smith – with tidings that the Governor and his cavalry had left Londinium heading south-west by the Noviomagus road, and taking many who would flee the city with him.

"One day sooner, and we should have caught the wolf in his lair," grumbled an old chieftain of the Cornovi.

But Boudicca said, "True enough. Yet it was not for catching the wolf in his lair that we came this way. It was for the sake of the Red Crests' weapons and stores – and for the tax-gatherers and the moneylenders and the fat merchants who made us lean and stripped our freedom from us. Some of our men have only hunting-spears, even sickles despite the spoils of Camulodunum, and we shall be better armed to hunt down this Governor of Britain, this wolf from his lair, after today's work be done. Harness up, my brothers, soon it will be dawn, and we head for Londinium."

So at first light, with the mist still hanging among the trees, we swept down from our ridge.

The outer skirts of Londinium were empty. No fighting from street to street as there had been at Camulodunum. Only one live thing I saw in those streets, save for the river gulls wheeling and crying like lost souls overhead, and that was a brindled cat who spat at us from the top of a wall. We quested down side-streets and into buildings as we went; but bath-houses and temples and the great Basilica and Forum stood up empty as though they belonged already to a city of the dead. Every living soul must have gathered to the supply depot. The river was empty too, no ships alongside the wharves and jetties; and the water was ruffled and blue under a fresh east wind that was rising.

So we headed for the great depot within its turf banks and palisades. And the only sound in all Londinium was the storm-roar of our coming.

Those who sought to defend the place had hacked down the bridge across the encircling ditch, and at the far side of the wreckage the gates stood up heavy-timbered and strong. But it did not take long to pull down the nearest wooden buildings, and fling in beams and shutters and roof-thatch to make a causeway. The defenders on the stockade-bank loosed off arrows and sling-stones at us, and in the dense battle-mass they could not fail to find their mark here and there; but few of them had good aim; and after we had flung in firebrands, and the smoke began to go up, where the stockade had caught, it gave us cover. The gate, too, we fired, piling burning thatch against it; but that was too slow, and a great beam torn from a nearby building served us better to batter the smouldering timbers down.

One man among the defenders on the stockade, we saw and lost and saw again and again, as the smoke drifted by. A tall man wearing a red leather cap such as some of the auxiliaries wear. He had a bow, and he knew how to use it, standing there on the crumbling breastwork between the smoke and the smoke, he loosed against the Queen herself, where she stood islanded in her chariot among the yelling hordes, and the arrow sped true, and would have taken her in the throat, but that her horses plunged sideways snorting from a firebrand even as it left the bow; so that it did no more than nick her upraised arm below the shoulder. It was but a wasp-sting, but those nearest to her saw the crimson line spring out on her skin, and the shout went up, "The Queen! The Queen is scathed! The Life runs out!" And the whole War Host surged forward against the gate and banks like a storm-wave pounding on a shingle ridge.

When at last we broke in, and the red spear-mark was done and over, we flayed the man in the red cap. We flayed three men who chanced to be wearing red caps, among the few who we took alive, to make sure. But truly, I do not think any of them was the right one. He was a very tall man, and none of their skins would have fitted him. I think, I hope, he was one of the fortunate ones who died in the fighting. The other captives we crucified – that is a thing that we have learned from the Romans themselves – and left them pegged out for the ravens, for a sign to the Red Crests if they came that way again. We took no heads. Save perhaps for the head of the tall man in the red cap, there were none worth taking. No warriors, only merchants and Government officials, and men of the Tribes who had turned traitor and grown fat following their Roman masters, and their women and their screaming children. . . .

Then we stripped the weapon store. The doors stood open, and many of the spears and even the short Roman swords had been taken by the folk to defend themselves. But that made no difference save that we took them from the dead instead of from the racks along the armoury walls. We took grain and wine and leather tunics, and all things that might be of use to us, and loaded them into the waiting ox-carts that came down for them. And then we fired the place behind us, very thoroughly. So that Londinium was a lake of flame from end to end and the smoke rolled like black storm-clouds across the evening sky.

And we came back to our camps along the wooded ridges, singing songs like a wolf-pack under the moon.

Next day, fast riders came from Andragius. "Verulamium is burned. The Red Crests are away south. Wait you till I come."

Two days, we waited, restless as ponies when the smell of wolf is in the wind; and in all those two days, no men, not even I who slept across her threshold, cared to risk our hides by speaking to the Queen. And then at evening, runners came with word that the Catuvellauni had returned and were making their camp to the west of us.

"Go then, and fetch the Prince Andragius to me," said the Queen, standing beside the fire that burned in the entrance to her black horse-hide tent. It was raining, I mind, and the horsehides were wetly shining, and the fine mizzle made a golden smoke as it eddied hissing into the fire.

"No need for that," said a voice, and Andragius with the blurred traces of the warpaint still on his cheeks, stepped with his light wildcat stride into the clearing.

The Queen turned on him. "What means this message of yours? You let the Red Crests break clear of your net?"

Andragius said, "No, for they never walked into our net. They never came to the place beyond Verulamium where the road is cut. Maybe the eagles of the sky told them of our war-bands on the move. They turned aside, somewhere up in the mid-lands, and went south through the gap in the High Chalk, heading for Calleva of the Atrebates."

"Did the eagles of the sky tell you all this?" the Queen said.

"We also have our Eyes and Ears out beyond the Host, to see and bring back tidings."

"Why did you not follow them up?"

"Lady, so deep into enemy territory?"

There was a silence. Only the drip of wet from the broad leaves of summer. Then Boudicca shook her head. "Na, that might well have been to run into a net in our turn. . . . You have not left the way open to them, if they should double back?"

He gave a snort of laughter, harsh and mocking behind his nose. "Lady, I was not chosen by the Catuvellauni to lead their war-bands because I could play the flute or weave rush baskets. The pass through the Chalk is held fast, until I give the word to pull back the men who hold it; and they are in fine fighting spirit, their hearts high and hot within them because we have laid flat to the blackened ground the city which the Romans raised upon the ruins of our own." But he spoke on a note of scorn for his own kind. And at a sudden roar of song and laughter from some distant part of the camp, he cocked his head. "As high as, it seems, are the hearts of the Iceni."

"Surely," the Queen told him. "For Londinium also lies flat to the ground, and the wolves and ravens make merry in the streets. Go now. Eat and rest. Tomorrow we will call together the chieftains, to decide the thing next to be done."

But after he was gone back to his own men, the Queen stood looking after him. And she said, broodingly, part to herself, part, I think, to me, "Their hearts are high and hot within them. They are drunk on revenge. Too drunk to know as I know, as Andragius of the War Cats knows, that we have been already twice too late. Too late to take the Governor in Londinium, too late to bring the Red Crests to battle in time and place of our choosing."

And then she laughed, flinging back her wild wet hair. "Yet what have we to fear? We have ten men to their one; and the Mother will not deny us the victory, for it is she who demands it!"

Mother dear, it is not many days since I last added to this letter; but it seems a very long time.

We pulled out of Londinium, and halfway down to Noviomagus along with the refugees. And the Governor sent urgent messages on with them, as a back-up to those he had already sent by galloper, appealing to Cogidubnos to raise as many "friendlies" as may be, and send them on up to us. They'll be only rough-riding cavalry and a few bowmen, but every little helps. Then we came back on our tracks, and here we are, encamped about eight miles south of Londinium and waiting for them to come; and, even more, waiting for reinforcements from Gaul. The Twentieth and Fourteenth have got through to us, by a roundabout way through friendly territory. So now our strength is up to something over eight thousand; but even so, we are many times outnumbered, and can only hope the Gaulish reinforcements come soon.

When I say we are encamped south of Londinium, we are encamped south of where Londinium used to be. It's just a vast black fire scar now, tastefully decorated with the remains of crucified men. Our scouts report that by the look of things the people in the depot must have put up quite a fight for it! Nothing moving now but the ravens and the carrion gulls. I suppose it makes a change from fish-guts. Oh Mother, I'm sorry; I only wrote that because I feel sick every time I think of that sprawling prosperous town. And now, if ever you read it, I shall have made you feel sick too. No I won't, I'll cross it out. When the legions got through to us, their scouts reported Verulamium in like case. That's three cities, and the gods know where it's going to end.

At the moment it seems that this Boadicea (that's the Queen's name) is encamped among the upland forests north of Londinium. She can't come south into enemy territory after us, and we haven't enough men to go north after her. It's like one of those horrible games when you get into a position where you can't make a move either way and you can't win. Though I suppose time is, if anything, on our side. At least we are likely to get the auxiliaries from Cogidubnos, and grow stronger, while if Paulinus is right, the Celts need to be used in hot blood to fight their best, and if kept waiting too long may even start to melt away. There are reports, too, that her people sowed no corn this spring, vowing to feed fat on our stores and harvest. So I suppose hunger might drive her from cover eventually. but it's not easy to feed even an army the size of ours, for long, sitting in one patch of country, with no depot and precious few lines of communication. So it looks as though we shall go nearly as hungry as she.

Later. Much later. It must be 2nd August I think. Still no reinforcements from Gaul. Seemingly there's some trouble and they can't easily be spared. I wish I knew if all is well with you; but they say the trouble isn't in the south.

I hope you can read this, my ink-stick is almost gone and I've mixed it weaker than usual to make it last out a bit longer.

14

The Corn Dancing

Yet again the Council Fire was lit, and the chieftains and war-captains gathered; and standing before them, Andragius of the Catuvellauni told again what he had told to the Queen beside her tent fire.

And when he had spoken, and the thing had been exclaimed at and snarled at and talked over – for the older I grow the more it seems to me that we of the Tribes must at all times do a great deal of talking – a chief of the Trinovantes said, "But what the Lord Andragius and his war-bands could not do, surely the whole War Host is strong enough to do! Now, therefore, let us harness up and cross the Father of Rivers and press on south after Suetonius Paulinus and his Red Crests!"

But Gretorix Hard-Council shook his grey shaggy head. "It is true that we outnumber the Red Crests many times; but even so, what gain shall it be for us to go hunting them into the territory of our bitterest foes? It would take us far from our own land, and if the Second Legion which is still in Glevum were to thrust eastward they could cut our road home behind us."

"What need have we of a road home?" demanded another chief. "Until all roads are free to us, and the Red Crests have been driven into the sea?"

So they talked on, one against another, until the Queen, who had sat listening, her eyes going to each speaker in turn, but saying no word of her own, spoke up at last. "Long have I listened to your words, O lords and chieftains and war-captains of the Tribes, now let you listen to mine. If we bide here, we can keep watch on all that the Red Crests do, and on every move that they make. Between the Father of Rivers and the Great Water, Paulinus must know that he is shut up as in a holding-pen. He must know that if ever his kind are to be the Lords of Britain again, he must come north of the river once more. Then we shall have him in our own hunting runs."

"How long can we bide?" a war-captain growled. "A War Host such as ours needs feeding."

"The land north of the river is empty of men but rich in corn and cattle," Boudicca said. "Rich pasture and good hunting shall feed the War Host as long as need be."

Then Tigernann of the Brigantes said, "The Bearers of the Blue Warshields fight best in hot blood." And his voice was insolent, and his thumbs again in his belt.

The Queen turned on him like a she-wolf, "Do we not all know the fighting ways of the Bearers of the Blue War-shields? All warriors of all tribes fight their best in hot blood! – Then let them bank up the heat, as the Women's Side smoore the fire at night for use again in the morning! Have we not learned to wait, we whose life is the corn and the herds? Who can hurry the growth of the seed-corn in the ground or the young in the belly of its dam? Yet the corn comes to harvest and the foal to birth in their own time – in the Mother's time. So shall it be with this waiting, and the red harvest that shall end it when the time of the Mother comes!"

And so, for upward of two moons we held our camps in the forest clearings, much where Caratacus must have waited for that last great battle with the Emperor Claudius, eighteen summers ago. We lived well enough at first, on the spoils of Londinium and the flocks and herds and garnered grain of the abandoned farms; and on the hunting, which is rich in those parts also.

But as time went by our foraging bands must push further and further afield for the lowing wild-eyed cattle that they drove back to the camps, and the hunting parties must quest deeper and deeper into the forest after deer and boar; and the granaries were low before ever we came to them, the year being close to harvest time again.

The harvest promised well enough, in the untended fields, but when the grain was heavy in the ear and beginning to turn colour, there came three days of wind and rain that tore and battered it down until much of it was scarce worth the gathering. We harvested the fields that were near enough, all the same, bringing in the draggled shocks of spelt and barley in the lightest of the big ox-wagons. They made a poor thin showing, and would not fill the bellies of such a War Host for long; but at least we could say that we had reaped and gathered in the captured harvest of the south. We who had sown no corn of our own in the spring.

And the women garlanded the wide horns of the oxen with scarlet poppies and corn marigolds and daisies of the moon, and danced before the ox-carts as they have always done. And when the last sheaf was cut, it was bound about with green leaf-sprays and coloured ribbons and drawn home in a lurching and swaying wagon by itself and with all honour as befits the Corn King.

In the days of our mothers' mothers the Corn King was a living man bound into the midst of the barley sheaf. But in these softer days it is most often only the shock of corn that is lauded and called King and then hacked to pieces by the women and ploughed back into next year's furrows. So it is at least with the Iceni. Other tribes, other customs.

So the Corn King on his wagon was drawn through the Queen's camp, and set up on a mound of turfs in the central clearing. And from all over, the Horse People gathered to the feasting. Some to the Royal Fire where the Corn King lolled on his turf throne, others to the lesser cook-fires scattered throughout the camp where the carcases of oxen slain that morning were roasting. And presently the folk feasted and the drink went round – wine from rich men's deserted farms, and barley beer that the women had brewed as best they could; raw stuff with a kick to it like a stallion. And throughout the camps of other tribes along the rolling forest country, much the same thing would be going on.

Some of the older warriors wagged their heads at so much feasting when there was no knowing how much longer we had to wait with our belts pulled ever tighter, before the Red Crests moved.

But food stored for the future is not the only thing needed to keep heart in a long-waiting War Host. Even I, who am no warrior but a harper know that. Maybe a harper knows it best. . . .

But that was no evening for waking the harp. Harping is for a Royal Hall, or for a few gathered beside a hunting fire under the stars, or for a Queen in her tent.

You cannot harp to a War Host. And after the eating was done and the drink jars going round, the women began to spill out onto the open space about the Royal Fire, where Boudicca had come from her long horse-hide tent to sit with the Princesses beside her. They joined hands, circling in the old secret patterns of the Corn Dance, to the music of reed pipes that grew always wilder and more shrill. And the quickening rhythms and the barley spirit set the blood on fire, and the pipes were calling, calling, until the Princesses left their places before the long black tent to join the dancers, eyes bright and hair and arms flying.

And then the wolfskin drums of the Men's Side took over from the flutes, and young braves sprang into the open space and began to whirl and stamp with upraised spears; and no one cared that it was a war-dance they made, and no dance for the Corn King at all; nothing mattered but the twisting and stamping and wild cries, and the fierce rhythms mounting like fever in the blood.

They laid bright patterns of naked swords on the turf that by now was almost trampled bare, and danced among them where one false step would have meant the loss of a foot. They pulled blazing branches from the fire crying, "We are the Sun that ripens the grain. Come, Harvest!" and drew the women out to join them in bright spinning sun-wheels of flame. I have seen many Corn Feasts in my time. But never the like of that Corn Feast. It seemed to me that the throbbing of the drums was the throbbing of my own heart, and the shrilling of the flutes made a white fire in my head; and the shadows of unknown things crowded out from the blackness of the trees, to make their own dark dancing just beyond the reach of the torches.

And then it was time for the death of the Corn King, and the women made for the shock of barley high on its turf throne. Chanting, they hacked off the heavy-eared head, and the grain scattered in a golden shower. They tore cornstalk from cornstalk until nothing of the King was left. And the whirling dance was stilled and the music of drums and flutes fallen silent and the dark shapes beyond the torchlight were gone.

Then, as it always happens after the Corn King is dead, the young braves began to catch at the hands of the girls who pleased them, and the girls to hold out their hands to the warriors of their choice; and together they ran away into the darkness beyond the reach of the fires. Always it ends so, the Corn Feast, and ten moons later, just as it happens ten moons after the Beltane Fires that welcome summer in, there are many children born among the Horse People.

Two young warriors, bright-eyed and laughing and flushed with the barley beer and the dancing, came running to where the two Princesses stood side by side. Essylt cried out furiously, a sharp screeching cry like a hawk, and struck furiously at the boy who would have caught her hands; and I saw as though in a slow dream – all things seemed to have gone slow – how Nessan, caught by the other, silently bent her dark head with the magic vervain flowers braided into it, and sank her teeth into the hand that grasped her wrist. The young warrior yelped with surprise and pain, but flung his other round her and forced her head up. And he was laughing still.

It was a thing that I had known must happen soon or late. In the old days, before the Procurator and his men came to the Royal Dun, no one save those who were named for them at the Choosing Feast would have thought to lay hands on the Royal Daughter or her sister. They were taboo, the channel through which the unbroken line of life, the life of the tribe, flowed on. But the Procurator and his Red Crests had come, and all that was changed. And the Queen also must have known the thing that would happen soon or late, and known also that if men came to use the Princesses as any other girls of the tribe, then that indeed would be the end of the Royal Line; maybe the end of the Tribe as well.

I looked to see what she would do.

She had risen from her seat, and stood with arms upraised. All round the Royal Fire, though I could hear the uproar of the Corn Feast going on through the rest of the camp and the camps beyond, a stillness began to spread. When it was complete, and every face turned towards her, she lowered her arms. But still she left the stillness unbroken. And no one but she could break it.

At last she said, not overloud, "Seize them."

And men of her bodyguard sprang forward to where the young braves stood with their hands dropped to their sides. Sober enough, they were now.

"Bring them to me," said the Queen.

And they were brought, their arms twisted behind them.

The Queen looked them over. "For overlong we have made this pretence, this token of Offering to the All Mother at Harvest time. And it is in my mind that the Mother grows weary of the pretence. Now, therefore, we will return to the old ways, and the Offering shall be a true one."

One of the young men licked his dry lips. The other

swallowed thickly. Neither made any attempt to break away.

"And this time we will make the Offering twofold."

The wolfskin drums were speaking again; but in a different tongue, a darker tongue that called for blood.

"Let them stand free," said the Queen. "They will not try to run."

The Princess Essylt stood as still as her mother, looking on. Her teeth showed between her lips. Her eyes were brighter than love could make them. But Nessan came running to fling herself down at her mother's feet.

"No!" she wailed, "Oh no, my mother, no! There has been enough of blood!"

And the Queen looked down at her with empty eyes. "Not yet. There has not even begun to be enough of blood. But soon that shall be set right."

And she made a sign to two of the bodyguard, and they drew their swords.

The two young warriors stood side by side, unmoving. The death spell was on them. I remembered how the black goat had stood for her to cut its throat, at the time of sending out the Cran-Tara.

And then, into the last heartbeat of time, there broke the sound of someone coming; a shifting and a splurge of voices beyond the firelight, and the Queen made a gesture to stay the men with the swords; and the drumming fell silent.

Into the light of the Royal Fire, shining with the sweat of his long running, came one of those hunters who were the Eyes and Ears of the War Host. He made for the Queen, and stood before her with heaving flanks.

"What word do you bring?" said the Queen.

"Lady, the Red Crests are making ready to break camp. They have already sent scouts on horses towards the upriver ford, and a strong party to hold for them the bridge at Londinos."

So the waiting was over at last.

"That is a good word," said the Queen. "The Corn Feast is ended, and we too will make ready to break camp." She turned back to the two young braves, and the men who stood with drawn swords beside them.

"So, I lend you back your heads. The Great Mother says that she will wait. This, I lay on you instead, that on the day of battle you shall bring me the head of Suetonius Paulinus, who calls himself Governor of Britain."

A long breath rose from the crowd about the fire. And the two young men looked at each other and laughed. They knew themselves still marked for death, by the task that had been laid on them, but it would be death in battle, which is better than to stand to have one's head struck off. I knew that even though we had the victory, I should not see them again.

Already the news was roaring through the camps, on and on along the forest ridges; and all night long there would be the throbbing and thrumming of the War Host making ready for battle.

This may be the last that I write to you, Mother. By this time tomorrow night, in one way or another it will all be over. We waited as long as might be for the reinforcements from Gaul – until it became clear beyond all doubt that they were not coming; and the supply situation was getting hopeless. So Paulinus decided to attack with what men he now has; about ten thousand counting the native cavalry and raw auxiliaries. And a couple of days ago we broke camp, and marched, some for Londinium Bridge, the rest of us for the river ford above the town. We had a sharp skirmish with a force of tribesmen at the ford – set there to slow us up, I suppose; they could have had no hope of stopping us. Felix was disembowelled under me. We had only known each other a few months, but he was a good fellow and I shall miss him. I took personal pleasure in killing the man who did it.

We spent last night in the old transit camp north of Londinium, then pushed on about a mile, to the place I think Paulinus has had in mind all the while, as giving us the best chance (if indeed we have any chance) of victory against odds of something like ten to one. A defile opening to the south-east, thickly wooded behind us and on either hand – really dense stuff, damp-oak and yew and thorn. The kind of stuff even the Britons can't attack through; though of course we have scouts out to guard against the impossible. Open scrub land in front. This is about the first time in history, I should think, that the Eagles have ever camped for the night without throwing up nice regular square banks and ditches. But as we shall fight tomorrow only just forward of where we sleep tonight, and we have the natural defence of the forest on flanks and rear, it seems better to leave the ground uncluttered. The Governor's pavilion has been set up in the centre of the camp with the Eagles and cohort standards ranged before it; and we have piled him a turf look-out platform for tomorrow, and that's all. Oh, and we've dug latrines. I think if the end of the world were at hand, we should prepare for it by digging latrines. Paulinus has been round from watchfire to watchfire talking to the men. The usual kind of thing, I should imagine. The honour of the Eagles, the honour of Rome, the whole future of Rome in Britain – remember that if they do outnumber us ten to one, they are an undisciplined rabble dangerous only in ambush and on ground of their own choosing, while we are disciplined troops packing ten times their fighting power man for man; and the fewer there are of us, the fewer there are to share the honour of tomorrow's victory. "So when the battle joins," says he, "keep close formation, and when your spears are thrown, out swords, and smash their faces in with your shield bosses." That bit got the biggest cheer.

That's about all. Now it's just the waiting. Not much use trying to get an hour's sleep. Paulinus doesn't sleep himself on the eve of battle, and doesn't see why any of his staff should either. Well I suppose we wouldn't anyway. The knowledge of Boadicea and her battle-host somewhere a few miles across that open country in the dark doesn't act as a lullaby. What a woman! I suppose if she has the victory tomorrow, they'll make a song about her to sing through Britain for a thousand years. They're a great people for making songs about their heroes, the British. If she has the defeat, too, come to think of it; only then it will be a lament.

I think I was nearly asleep, then, after all. Better get up and walk around a bit.

15

Red Harvest

The War Host rolled out from the forest and turned south and west towards the ruins of Londinium. As many as though the leaves of the forest had fallen and turned into warriors. Men on foot and on horseback and in chariots, with their spears thirsty again after the long wait; and bringing up the rear, the great ox-wagons with the women and children and the Priest Kind; the Royal Wagon lurching along like a ship on dry land in their midst; and the Queen with the chariot columns at the head of all.

There is a place, where the forest comes down towards Londinium – towards where Londinium used to be. A valley runs up into it from the open scrub land; and the rising flanks and the high ground at its head are matted thick with trees; yew and thorn and dense dwarf oak, with scarce a deerpath to make a way through it. And when word was brought to the Queen that the Red Crests were camped there for the night, no more than ten thousand, counting the renegade tribesmen they call auxiliaries, and their cavalry which has always been a jest to the horsemen of the Iceni, she laughed, and said, "Surely their gods have made them mad, that they have set themselves down in a trap, and we not having to lift a finger to drive them into it!"

That night we made our own camp scarce three Roman miles short of the place. And next morning, when the sun rose and the mists scarfed the river valley, and the dew of late summer spattered from the bracken as the horses' legs brushed by, we went forward on the last stretch. We were like a great shadow spilling along the land, the shadow of a vast storm-cloud, made up of men and horses, stretching back as far and wide as the eye could see. And out of the storm-darkness came the rolling thunder of wheels and hooves and tramping feet, and the lightning that the level sun-rays struck from spear-points and horse-trappings and the captured cohort standards that we carried with us.

So we came in sight of the valley, and our lightnings were answered by the sun-flash on Roman spears and helmets and on the great spread-winged eagle standards that waited for us. We seemed borne along towards them on our own spread-wings of storm; not fast, we could not move fast with the lurching wagons drawn by their straining teams of oxen in the rear. But there was no hurry. We held them penned. Corralled like cattle for the slaughter. And they crowed defiance at us with their silver trumpets as we drew nearer, and our great war-horns boomed hollow in reply.

The morning-shadows of men were still tree tall on the rough grass when we rolled to a halt, and spread out into a vast new-moon curve all across the open ground before the mouth of the valley, the Tribes ranged each under its own chiefs and war-captains; the foot-spears and the horsemen, the chariot columns in the midst, the great wagons drawn up in the rear, and the oxen turned free to graze. There was no hurry. It was close on noon before we were done with our ready-making. And all the while, the Red Crest ranks drawn up in the mouth of the clearing sat on their haunches or stood leaning on their spears, and watched us, their cavalry horses fidgeting and neighing to ours, who fidgeted and neighed back again. They were so few, the men in the Red Crest lines; so few that it scarce seemed worth unleashing the whole War Host against them, save that those held back would have risen up in fury at being denied their part in the kill.

And all the while, the Queen in her chariot, with the Princesses following in another, drove to and fro, taking the reins herself, and reining in her dancing team to speak to the men of this tribe and that: the Brigantes, the Cats of War, our own Horse People.

"I would bid you see how few they are," she said. "But what are their numbers to us? We are a proud people fighting for our own. Think of the freedom they robbed us of, and that will be ours again, and I promise you the fight will be a short one, and before the time comes to kindle this evening's cooking-fires, we shall have avenged old wrongs and be our own lords again!"

And everywhere the men laughed and shouted for her, "Boudicca! Boudicca!" and brought their spears crashing down across their shields in salute.

Then she came back to the Royal Wagon, and the Princesses got down from their chariot to wait among the Women of the Kindred. They were not to ride with her into the battle, so that, if death came for her in the time of victory, the Royal blood would still be there and the Line of Life unbroken, and the Horse People not left without a Queen.

Chiefs and captains came and went about her; and the sun stood at noon; and the Prince Andragius sent her word, "It is time to give the Order."

And she sent back word, "There is time enough

before the cooking-fires. They have made us wait long enough; let them sweat a while."

There was a little hillock to the far right of our battle curve; a few thorn bushes on its crest; and there the Priest Kind had gathered, with oak garlands on their heads. They stood with arms upraised and made the ritual gestures, chanting in the ancient tongue, their feet never moving, as though they, like the thorn trees, were rooted there. And Boudicca stood there also, looking out towards the enemy, while her red chariot ponies fidgeted and fretted just below, tossing their heads and swishing their tails against the gadflies that hung in stinging swarms above the chariot lines.

And I too was there. I would have been among the fighting men, my harp left safe in the Royal Wagon, but Boudicca said, "Na, na, my Harper. If you go down amongst the fighting, you will know nothing of the battle but the three men nearest to you; and like enough a spear in your throat. And how then shall you make me my great Song of a Queen's Victories that shall be sung round our hearths for a thousand winters? Let you bide here, and see all things as they happen from the beginning to the end."

And then a thing happened that was strange indeed. Out from the scrub close by broke a hare, just as I have seen them break from the corn before a line of reapers. The hare that is sacred to all the Tribes whether they be Stag People or Horse People or Cats of War. Close before the hillock it checked and sat up on its haunches; and I saw the beauty of it, the full, light-bloomed eye, the sunlight striking through its long quivering ears, that flushed them deeper than a dog-rose and showed every delicate branching vein within. For a breath of time it seemed to be looking at the Queen; then with a thrust of its powerful hind legs it sprang forward and went racing straight along our battle line.

A great roar of triumph went up from the waiting warriors; and the Queen cried out like a trumpet above the surge of their voices, "The Mother is with us! All our gods are with us! Now – forward and break them!"

She swung up her father's sword, and it seemed to me that jagged shards of light broke from the blade in the heat-hazed sunshine, and with a bellowing of war-horns the charge broke forward.

And from the little hillock where she had bidden me wait, I saw, Grief upon me! I saw all things as they happened, from the beginning, far on towards the end.

The Roman trumpets were yelping, and far off in the Red Crests' lines, the men who had been sitting or leaning on their spears, had straightened to become an unbroken wall of shields. And towards them our chariot line rolled forward, slowly at first, the ponies fighting for their heads, then gathering speed and power and terror. I felt the ground throbbing under my feet with the drum of hooves and the fury of chariot wheels as the great curved line swept on towards that waiting wall of Red Crests. I saw men and horses going down to right and left beneath the first flight of Roman spears, but the rest thundering on to crash into the ranks that stood like a rampart to receive them. I saw great ragged holes suddenly appear in the foremost rampart, and the chariots pouring through to hurl themselves on another that lay behind it. And the dust-cloud began to rise, and I could scarcely hear the roar of the joined battle for the baying of our own foot-spears, like hounds in leash who sight the quarry. In one place, two, maybe more, the chariots broke through again. Then came a check. There must have been a third line, and it must have held; and then out of the turmoil the chariots came again, heading back towards the Tribes. Something over half way, they wheeled about and hurled forward again, our horsemen flanking them, upon the Roman lines that had scarce had time to reform.

And the bright yelping of the trumpets and the booming of the war-horns rose and flung to and fro above the storm-roar of battle. And this time, I looked to see the chariots break clean through. Nearer and nearer they swept until they seemed almost upon the waiting Red Crests. And then in the last instant before the shock of meeting, their centre seemed to tear wide open like a horrible red wound. Horses were down and threshing, dragging their chariots with them; and the second wave of chariots, too close to pull clear, went crashing headlong into them, making a still more hideous confusion. The air above it was dark and thrumming with spears and sling-stones from the forward surging mass of our own foot warriors; and under the dark hail, suddenly the shape of the enemy was changing. From the straight three-fold rampart that it had been, it was becoming a wedge. A vast, terrible shield-flanked wedge, fanged and taloned with ripping sword-blades, driving into the gap that their spears had torn open for them, and thrusting on – and on. . . .

The Red Crest trumpets were screaming like angry hawks above the battle-roar; the shouted war-cries and the shrieks of horses and the crash of splintering chariots.

The Queen was away down from her watch place on

the hillock. She sprang into her chariot, and screamed something, there was no hearing what, to her charioteer. I saw him jab in the goad, and the horses sprang forward, scattering blood from their pierced haunches. The Queen's standard-bearer galloped beside her. She was waving up the last reserves of chariots. I saw them hurtling forward like a winter skein of wild geese – to meet the remains of the second chariot charge that were streaming back. I wondered whether she could turn them yet again, and if not, whether she would be caught up and engulfed by them in their flight. But I did not wait to see. I slipped my harp-bag from my shoulder and hung it on a thorn branch, for the time of the harp was past, and dropped down from the hillock, drawing my sword as I ran. A wild-eyed and riderless horse swept by me, and I caught it, and headed after the Queen for the boiling heart of things.

And then for a while, even as she had said, I knew little more of the battle than the three men nearest me. My throat was full of the smell of blood and sweat and the choking dustcloud out of which men and horses reeled to and fro. I had lost all sight of the Queen, all knowledge of where she was, so that I could no more be following her. The struggle had lost all shape and pattern and sense; but somewhere in the heart of it, driving on and on, I knew was that terrible wedge-shaped beast – in my mind it had become a beast, not a formation of mortal men – that the Red Crests had unleashed against us. and gradually, through the dust and the red trampling chaos, I became aware of other things. Fresh waves of the enemy pressing in on us from the wings, cavalry bursting in upon our close-packed foot warriors, hacking their way through so that the tribesmen went down like barley before the reapers.

Our battle mass was being cut to rags – separate, desperate bands of men gathered about a chieftain or a standard, dying where they fell among the still-threshing legs of wounded chariot ponies. And slowly, relentlessly, the whole shapeless battle beginning to move one way. Between those little cut-off steadfast bands, the lesser men were streaming back. Panic is a strange and terrible thing, and when it strikes it is as catching as the yellow sickness. Suddenly all around me men were running, with wide eyes and open mouths, some even flinging their spears away. I was caught up in the wave and swept backward – backward towards the wagons drawn up in our rear. And then I understood what those wagons would mean; the oxen turned out to graze, so that even if there had been time, they could not be dragged clear. It was not the Red Crests, but we, who were in the trap.

I had only one thought after that, to reach the Royal Wagon and the Princesses. What good I thought I could do, I would not be knowing. I got my chance-come horse turned about, and drove him towards where I could still see the red horse-tail pennants hanging in the still air above the roof of the Royal Wagon. I was almost there when a flung spear took him in the throat, he reared up, screaming through his own blood, then came crashing to the ground. I managed to fling clear as he fell, and ran on. More than once I think I used my sword on my own kind to clear my way through. And then at last I had gained the place that I made for.

All along the line the women were making frenzied

efforts to drag the wagons round, to make space between them. But it was hopeless, even if there had been time. There would be escape for some on the furthest flanks of the fighting, round the ends of the wagon line; if they had been coming in a thin trickle there would have been a way out under the floorboards and between the wheels. But what was sweeping down on them was a vast wave of men, dense-packed and desperate, with the hunters hard behind.

Some of the foremost swarmed under and ran free; the rest turned at bay, weaponed or weaponless, there being nothing else to do; men and women, and even the children with a stone or an arrow or a dead man's dirk.

And so the Red Crests burst upon us with their short stabbing swords.

Around the Royal Wagon, a few of us from the Kindred made our last rallying point, the Queen's women fighting among us. I mind the Princess Essylt clinging to the side of the wagon itself, one foot on a wheel-hub, a dead man's sword in her hand, her red hair flying about her head, fighting like a wild cat and chanting some savage war-song of her own as she struck, and struck again, until a legionnaire's sword, stabbing upward, took her beneath the breast-bone, and her song broke into a scream as she tumbled down into the struggling tangle below.

Nessan was beside me, with a dirk for her weapon. Even in that moment she cried my name, as though my coming meant rescue, safety, something to be glad for.

The shouting and screaming rose to tear the skies asunder; the Red Crest cavalry swept in with their long sabres to aid the men of the short swords cutting down every living thing, man, woman, child and horse, that came in their path. They had three cities, and four cohorts of the Ninth Legion to avenge, and the dead began to lie thick, hacked and hideous, piled one upon another.

A Red Crest with half his shoulder-guard torn away came leaping over the barrier of the dead. I lunged forward to meet and turn his sword; and in the same heartbeat of time a cavalry man crashed by, crouched low in the saddle, his long blade sweeping out and down, and Nessan fell against me and crumpled to my feet. My own sword had found its mark; I wrenched it out, feeling it grate on bone as the Red Crest went over backwards, and when I looked down, Nessan was lying twisted with her face turned to the sky and blood welling from a deep wound between her neck and shoulder.

I saw that she called out to me, though I could not hear above the tumult. Her eyes clung to my face, and she made as though she would hold her arms out to me as she used to do when she was a very small child.

And I knew that the battle was lost; and it seemed to me as in a dream, that all I had to do now was to save the child. I slammed home my sword into its sheath, and stooped and heaved aside the bodies that clogged my feet. There was a small clear gap between the wheels of the wagons. If I could get her through it into some kind of shelter, when the slaughtering was over and the darkness came, I might be able to get her away.

She was very light to lift; but even as I knelt with my arms round her, a moment of blinding pain took me in the left flank, in the soft unguarded part between ribs and hip. I pulled out the light spear-head, and my strength seemed to come with it, like water. I flattened on top of her, and lay still. Somewhere above us in the wagon a woman screamed loud enough to tear through even that turmoil. The taste of blood came into my mouth, and every instant I waited for the death blow, not yet knowing that in truth I had it already. But the Red Crests ploughed on, shouting as they thrust and thrust again. And in the breathing space that followed, I gathered myself and dragged Nessan further in under the wagon, and again lay down over her.

And from somewhere deep within me rose the half memory of thunder over the marshes, and Prasutagus flinging himself over Boudicca in the path of the stampeding horse-herd. And then for a while everything became like a dream, full of tumult and cries and confusion, that had neither time nor place nor meaning.

I came back to myself a long while later. The noise of fighting had gone away into a great silence. Only a ragged cry here and there with long gaps between, only the sounds of running and scrambling feet that went and came and went again, and somewhere a man shouting to another in the Roman tongue, as the Red Crests went about their looting. Somewhere a wolf howled; and the day had long since turned to dusk and the dusk deepened into the dark.

There began to be a new light, red and fitful, and a crackling sound, they were firing the wagons with their piles of dead. Red light slanted through the gaps in the floorboards above me. The Royal Wagon was ablaze, and burning fragments began to fall all round me.

I thought that I must get the child clear. The fire

seemed to reach in at me through the wound in my flank, as I lifted myself off her. But I could move. The ground under my hands was sodden with blood; her's, or mine, or a mingling of both. She lay very still. The flame-glare from the next wagon slanted in between the wheels, and warmed the colour of her skin, and her eyes were wide and looking up at me; but she lay exactly as I had set her down, and surely she was very still.

"Come, little bird," I whispered stupidly. "Wake! It is time to be away!" I would get her out on the far side of the wagon; and if we could get clear of the flame-light before we were seen, the night would cover us.

"Nessan!" I said. "Nessan! Wake now!" For my wits were still half gone.

And then I saw that she was dead.

I took her by her shoulders and pulled her still further under the burning wagon, so that when it fell in it would cover her and take her with it, beyond the reach of the Red Crests. I laid her straight and seemly as best I could, drawing the heavy braids of her hair down either side of her face and onto her breast, straightening her torn skirts down to her feet. I unsheathed my sword – I still had a knife, and that was all the weapon I should need now – and folded her hands on the hilt. Not because it was a sword; she was not her mother – but for a parting gift, because it was mine. If I had had my harp with me, I would have left her that instead. A timber fell beside us with a shower of sparks, and one side of the wagon settled a little.

I crawled out between the wheels on the far side, the side away from the day's battle; and left her to the flames.

It is all over. And I can't quite believe it, Mother.

We have pulled back to the old transit camp; and I suppose we shall be here for a day or two, while we bury our dead – we have surprisingly few – and get our wounded sorted out, and see to all the things that have to be seen to after a battle.

Paulinus drew up the line-of-battle troops in three ranks, one behind the other, across the mouth of the valley, with the auxiliaries and cavalry on the wings. Our spears took a fairly heavy toll of the first chariot charge; but they managed to break clear through the front rank, even so, and tear a few holes in the second, before the third flung them back. But when the second charge came on, our men had orders to hold until the last moment, and then make their throw all towards the centre of the enemy line. They carried out their orders splendidly, and tore a great gap in the centre; and we formed a wedge and drove through it into the very heart of the British battle-mass; after which the auxiliaries and cavalry closed in from the wings. It was hot work for a while, but eventually we got them on the run. – Only they couldn't even run; they had parked their wagon train straight across their line of retreat. Jupiter! They must have been sure of victory! – And we cut them to pieces against their own wagons.

The troops spent most of the night looting. They killed everything that moved; man, woman, child, war-pony, even the draught oxen from the wagons, and then fired the ruins. Paulinus doesn't usually allow that kind of thing, I'm told; but he made no attempt to stop them.

Boadicea seems to have escaped; but there's no more she can do; no danger to the Province any more. We had a terrific victory. They're beginning to say that we killed eighty thousand British for the loss of only four hundred of our own men. But I'd take that with a grain of salt. I very much doubt if there were eighty thousand in the whole War Host; and we took prisoners enough to flood the slave market, this winter. And of course, despite the wagon line, quite a lot must have got away.

Everything feels a bit flat, now. But I imagine that we shall have plenty to do later. Paulinus sacrificed on the Altar of Vengeance when he had made the more orthodox offerings after the battle; and intends to make a thorough job of seeing that nothing like this ever happens again, if he has to wipe out what remains of the Iceni and about six other tribes, and burn down half the Province to do it.

If ever I am Governor of Britain, I hope I never have anything like this to handle!

Mother dear, I've kept my promise to write, after a fashion. But I have suddenly decided I shan't send this letter. There are things in it better not written lest the wrong eyes should read them. And things that will make you worried and sad. It's dirty, too. I've carried it in my saddle-bag all this while, and there's blood on it. I'll write you a nice clean letter with no blood on it, when I have more time. Or maybe I'll wait till I get leave and can tell you the story myself.

There's a good fire burning in front of the Governor's pavilion. Sylvanus – another of the Staff

Tribunes, and normally rather an exquisite young man – is trying to roast a hare over it on the point of a spear. I shall drop this into the hottest part of it, and watch the papyrus crumble away.

Your loving, tired, dirty and hungry son
Gneus Julius Agricola

16

"Sleep Now, You and I"

I looked back once, and saw the ragged fringe of flame leaping up from the burning wagons. The horsetail pennants of the Royal Wagon had become tassels of flame, and there was a woman hanging head-down over the side, among blazing rags of embroidered horsehide. And my ears were full of the sounds of sack and pillage. Somewhere the wolf howled again. I half ran, crouching low, for a patch of thorn scrub, and lay full length in the shelter of it, until I had snatched back enough breath to go on. There were moving shadows in the night, running, lurching, crawling on hands and knees. I joined them, making for the dark refuge of the forest.

Away at the end of the wrecked wagon line, I passed close by the little hillock with its crest of thorn trees, and left it to its dead priests. I did not go seeking my harp hanging from its thorn branch. There would be no more harp-song.

Yet was on my forehead that I was the Queen's Harper still; for on the forest verge, in the shelter of a jagged earth hollow under the roots of a tree that had been blown down in some past gale, I stumbled among a little knot of men. One of them had me by the hair, his knife cold at my throat before I well knew it; but another caught his arm and cursed him for a fool who could not tell a Red Crest from another of themselves. And he let me go. And I knew from the sound of the tongue that I was among my own tribe.

There were four of them, black shapes in the lesser dark. And a fifth lay still in their midst, muffled in a cloak. A woman's shape I thought, even then; her face a pale blur like something floating under the surface of dark water; and bending close, I knew the truth even before one of them said, "It is the Queen."

I put my hand under the breast folds of her cloak, thinking to feel the stillness of death, but the life in her was still beating.

"We found her against the northern flank," said another, "lying across the wreck of her chariot. The charioteer must have been killed and the horses bolted. She had bound the reins round her waist, to have her hands free for her sword. There's no mark on her save a broken place – here – running out of her hair."

"The Mother of Foals turned the eyes of the Red Crests away, and we were able to bring her off, round the end of the wagon line," said the third.

And the fourth said, broodingly, "She promised us the victory."

There were a few ponies who must have escaped the same way, running loose among the scrub; for the Red Crests, though they had butchered every living thing among the wagons, had not given chase. Maybe they thought too few had escaped to make it worth their while. We managed to catch two, and got the Queen up onto one of them. She lay heavy in my arms as one newly dead, and when I would have lifted her up, the wound under my ribs pulled me back as with ropes. Two other men took her from me, and lifted her up and over, while I crouched coughing on the ground.

"How sore is the hurt? Can you travel?" someone asked.

I knew what that meant. If I could not get away with them, they would kill me to save me from a slow death or falling into Roman hands, according to the custom of the Tribes. But I was not done with my life yet. Not while Boudicca lived and might have need of me. I shook my head, my breath coming back. "A spear-hole under the ribs. It's not deep. I'll do well enough if I can stop the bleeding."

The Queen fell forward along the pony's mane, and they bound her hands together under its neck with broad strips torn from her cloak, to help keep her from falling off, while I made shift to lash myself tight about the middle with a strip torn from my own. Then we dragged ourselves into weary movement, and straggled off along the woodshore, until in the first grey light of dawn we found a deer track leading northward into the depths of the trees. So we set out to carry the Queen home.

Two of us walked all the while beside the pony to steady her on its back, the other three straggling behind with the second pony. At most times I was one of those who walked beside the Queen; the others accepted that it was my right when I told them that I was of her household; and in steadying her, I could steady myself against my own weakness that made all things hazy and my feet seem very far away. Once or twice I rode the second pony for a while, but he was a chariot beast, and not good for riding, and for the most part we tried to keep him fresh in case of a greater need.

Somewhere about the Trinovantes' border, we came on a deserted farm, and killed a half-starved pig.

We made a little fire, though we dared not raise much smoke for fear of who or what might come to it, and feasted on scorched flesh, and even contrived to get a little blood-broth down the Queen's throat. She seemed able to swallow though she gave no sign of being aware. And questing through the small turf-roofed huddle of buildings, we found other things that were of use to us; among them an old cloak to replace the Queen's that, though ragged now, was all too brightly scarlet. And for me, more rags to bind over the hole in my flank that oozed redly all the while. If I could stop the bleeding, I thought through a haze, I could maybe hold back the growing weakness until we got the Queen home to her own place again.

But the best thing we found in the place was a farm sledge, old and rickety; no more than a shallow hurdlework box on clumsy runners; but we piled bracken into it and harnessed up the chariot pony as best we could, and laid the Queen within. And after that we had better travelling, save when the sledge got bogged down in soft places or once when it was nearly swept away at a river ford.

Other people began to come and go in the fiery mist that was all about me. The wild country was full of fugitives; never many together for on the run, especially in familiar country, a handful do better than a large band. A few joined themselves to us, all the same. None that I knew, and now I cannot remember their faces, and I am doubting if they will remember mine. We were shadows cast together, no more.

We pushed on, living on the country as best we could; a country that was already stripped bare; and lay up for a few hours from time to time, not because it was night, or because it was day, but because we had come to some spot where there was grazing for the two wretched ponies, or a corner of a ruined bothie to make a shelter for the Queen.

Sometimes, as my weakness grew on me and the wound seemed to strike deeper, I rode beside her for a while; the sledge was big enough for two, though it made hard work for the pony, and the men on the hauling ropes. I could earn the ride by holding her against the jolting of the rough way. And one day, as I crouched, holding her so, against my knee, I felt her stir, and when I looked down her eyes were open. She had opened them not long after we first set out, but they had been only holes in her face. Now she was looking out of them, looking up at me, not yet knowing where she was, or why; and the dark forests had gone from behind them, and once again she was the Boudicca I knew.

She stirred again, and felt my arm about her, and said, "Cadwan?"

"I am here," I said.

"Do you remember how you carried me home in your cloak, when I had run away to follow my father against the cattle raiders?"

The man leading the sledge pony looked back over his shoulder.

"I remember," I said.

And after a while, she asked, "Where is my father's sword?"

"Here beside you." I lifted it and put the hilt in her hand, but she let it fall back into the bracken.

She looked about her, seeing the sledge and the wretched ponies, and the men looking like their own ghosts padding alongside. And her eyes came back to my face; a little frown between them. She did not ask of the battle. She had no need to. "The children? What of – the children?"

"Dead," I said, "both dead. All dead. Sleep now, Lady." For she was still too near some shadowy borderland for the words to have full meaning for her.

I do not know if she slept, but she closed her eyes, and said no more for a long time.

We came at last, skirting the cold ruins of Camulodunum, across the frontier runs into our own land again. A land almost bare of people in its southern stretches, though at least we were able to get a few scrub ponies in place of our two that were almost done. Most of the people who were left had gone into hiding, driving the best of the herds with them into the forest fastnesses. And the few who remained seemed stunned, and looked at us with sullen and even hostile eyes; for the news of the battle had gone through days ahead of us. But they gave us food; warm water and fresh rags for our wounds; only no shelter anywhere, lest the Red Crests should come.

The sledge fell to pieces days ago; but by then, Boudicca was strong enough to ride again. We found her a mare with a foal at foot, and a woman at the door of a half-ruined steading gave us an old riding-rug to fling across her back. She was a valiant one, that woman, she helped the Queen to wash the dried blood from her hair and let us stay long enough for her to half dry it at the hearth fire. Then we rode on, Boudicca in our midst, her damp bright hair spread loose on her shoulders, looking always straight ahead of her towards the place where she would be.

We had thought at first to take her off into hiding, but she would not have it so. She would go back to the Royal Dun.

"That is madness!" I said. "Soon the Red Crests will be everywhere, but above all, they will be at the Royal Dun."

And she smiled, gently, as though at the foolishness of a child, and said, "I shall be away before the Red Crests come."

And so, yesterday, a little before sunset, we brought her home up the track to the empty gateway of the Dun.

Another stretch of the Hall roof has fallen in since we went south, and the Wild has flowed further in. There was a smell of fox about the place; but there was a little fire burning on the upper of the two hearths, and the feel of people about, and as we dropped from the backs of the weary ponies before the threshold, Old Nurse came through the doorway from the women's quarters, like a withered leaf that a puff of wind might blow away.

Boudicca turned from the foal she had been fondling, and which instantly ducked its nose under its mother's flank and began to suckle, and walked towards her, and Old Nurse opened her arms and gathered her in.

"I have come home," Boudicca said.

"Aiee! You have come home. The word went by many sunsets ago; and I knew that you would come. So I have made a fire for you, and spread fresh rugs on the bedplace."

"Have you any food for the few who come with me?"

"Surely," said the old woman. "But I did not come back from hiding alone; others will see to their wants. Come now to the fire, and rest, and also eat."

"I will come to the fire," Boudicca said, "for I am

cold. So cold. But it is not for food that I come home to you; it is that I may drink the Sleep-Drink in the place where I was born. You have the needful herbs? Go now and brew it for me, Nurse Dear."

"It is already brewed," said Rhun. "For that also, I knew."

And she went back the way she had come. And the Queen sat down on the pile of skins beside the fire, holding out her hands to the warmth, for a faint mist was rising with the sunset, and the first chill of autumn was in the air. I bided on my feet beside her, with my arm round the nearest of the great roof-trees to hold myself from falling. For now that the journey was over, it was in my mind that if I once sat down, in my rightful place, the Harper's place at her feet, I should never rise again, and I was still not quite done with my body.

"Now you will never make me my Great Song to match with my Great Sword," Boudicca said, "my Song of a Queen's victories."

I shook my head, and the Hall blurred round me. "You have had the Great Sword. The Little Song will have to do."

"A little song, and a sword made of white willow wood," she said; and began to sing, very softly as though to the fire:

> " . . . Now the light fades
> And the wild duck home are winging,
> And sleep falls like dew from the quiet sky.
>   'Sleep now,' says my sword,
>   'Sleep now, you and I.'"

The rough curtain over the entrance to the women's quarters was drawn aside, and Old Nurse came back, carrying the wonderful cup of Roman glass that had been Prasutagus's third Bride Gift.

It was half full of some colourless faintly cloudy liquid, and the Queen rose, and took it between her hands, and stood a few moments gazing down into the depths of it, beyond the dried hemlock flowers that floated on the surface. And as she did so, I saw the light from the little fire catch and kindle the sleeping flame in the heart of the cup, so that from its dark, dusty, end-of-summer green it flowered into a glory of shadowy gold and flame, all the smouldering colours of a wild sunset.

Then she raised it, and drank to the last drop, and let the cup fall with a crash onto the hearth stone and shatter into a hundred fragments.

She stood very still, as though savouring what she had done. Then, to Old Nurse, she said, "Go now. And presently, bring the other women you have with you to the Royal Chamber." And to me, she said, "Do not think me greedy that I have drunk it all. Old Nurse will go back to her own kind. And you? You have no need of the Sleep-Drink. Do you think I do not know how you have fought to stay in your body all these journey days, that you might be with me while I still had need of you? You have only to cease the fighting and go free."

Then she put her hands on either side of my face, and kissed me on the forehead. I felt her lips already cold through my own rank sweat. "The sun and the moon on your path, Cadwan of the Harp. When you hear the women keening, you will know that I have made my peace with the Mother. You will know that I am beyond the Red Crests' reach, and shall not be dragged in chains like Caratacus, to add splendour to a

Roman triumph. Then go free, and be done with the weariness and the pain."

And she turned, gathering her father's sword once more into her arms, and walked away, like a Queen still, up her ruined Hall. In the doorway of the Royal Chamber, she swayed a little, then steadied herself and walked on, and the rough curtain fell to behind her.

Then I took the last of my strength as it were in both hands, and dragged my way out here into the apple garth, where I have made so many songs to sing by firelight, and shall make no more. And let myself lie down at last, in the long grass against the little that is still left of the old half-fallen tree. The mist was wreathing up from the lowland pastures, and the little white moon-moths fluttering star-pale among the branches in the dusk.

That was a long while ago, when I was still Harper to a Queen. Or maybe not so long. I do not know. A while since, I heard the women keening.

Not any more.

Nothing any more.

Author's Note

It was in two books of T. C. Lethbridge's, *Witches* and *Gog-Magog*, that I first came upon the theory that the Iceni were a matriarchy: the royal line, and with it the life line of the tribe, descending from mother to daughter. So that Boudicca was their Queen in her own right, and Prasutagus their King only because he was her husband.

That was often the way, among the older Iron-Age peoples. And if it was so in this case, then, to the tribe's way of thinking, it would turn the Romans' treatment of the Queen and princesses from brutal tyranny into something much worse, into sacrilege against the Life itself. And it would turn what followed from tribal revolt into Holy War; which of all wars is the most savage and merciless kind.

Also, in some odd way, it seemed to me to turn Boudicca into much more of a real person. And real people, lost behind their legends, have always fascinated me.

The result, many years after first reading *Witches*, is *Song for a Dark Queen*.

Of the books I searched through, trying to get the story straight, Lewis Spence's *Boadicea* gave me the most help with the actual revolt, and the Roman campaign that finally crushed it. And from *Agricola and Roman Britain* by A. R. Burn, I learned what I think I should have known before: that Gneus Julius Agricola, who, nearly twenty years later, was the greatest Governor Roman Britain ever had, was a young tribune on the staff of the Governor Suetonius Paulinus, in fact his "tenting companion", which is to say his personal aide-de-camp, throughout the campaign.

One thing more. Alas, there were no scythe blades on the wheels of the British war chariots. When one comes to think of it, in a mêlée they would have removed the legs of their own side just as efficiently as they would have removed those of the enemy.